Lisa Marie Cochrane is a new author who explored her love of writing during the early phase of the Covid lockdown. Embellished diary entries soon became chapters which soon became a story. Her Scottish voice can be heard and echoed in the book itself. She lives outside Falkirk with her family and loves exploring her hometown and all its gems.

To my wonderful friends and family who helped shape the story with their encouragement, interest and time taken to read my words. Thank you.

Lisa Marie Cochrane

CRY BABY

AUSTIN MACAULEY PUBLISHERS™

LONDON • CAMBRIDGE • NEW YORK • SHARJAH

A CIP catalogue record for this title is available from the British Library.

ISBN 9781398433298 (Paperback)
ISBN 9781398433304 (ePub e-book)

www.austinmacauley.com

First Published 2022
Austin Macauley Publishers Ltd®
1 Canada Square
Canary Wharf
London
E14 5AA

1. 18 March 2018

The 18th of the month. The slowest Monday of them all. Long gone were the eager spenders celebrating payday and filling their boots with cheap half*s* before moving on to the brighter scenes of the town centre. Their return to the bar seemed ages away and for now, it was the handful of regulars Teeny would be stuck with, listening to the usual moans and drivels of them breaking up their painfully boring days by spending a few hours in the pub.

"Am fuckin tellin' ye, Rab, it was a photo finish, Mel's Diner should've had it. Pish! £23 I could've had back there."

"Right, Teeny, another pint eh heavy…in the Carling glass though hen and a Black Heart for Stuarty – jist two wee bits eh ice, no big wans."

Not that she needed the extra direction. Rab and Stuarty had been drinking in the Cross Keys since she was small enough to come into the pub and climb onto their laps and help them choose horses based on which jockey had the prettiest jumper whenever her dad was in having a cheeky jar instead of taking her to the park, which was all too often. She would gleefully drink her fizzy juice with a fancy straw and umbrella and eat her cheese and onion crisps licking her fingers so she could trace down the patterned images in the

7

newspaper and felt like she was the most important person in the room.

"Teeny Bash, Queen of the Cross Keys."

The nostalgia now made her shudder looking at the sad old men who now commented on how low her top would be cut or that the boots she was wearing were for 'girls who enjoyed the boaby'. A sickly trickle of shame crept 'round her neck when she pictured herself sitting on the men's knees all those years ago. Had she imagined their hands on her thighs under her yellow dress? Did it suit them more than her father to keep the little pigtailed girl occupied while her father drank himself into a stupor? The scenes flashed between the yellow dress, the rows of pound coins for more crisps and juice and the rows of jockey sweatshirts in the newspapers. She shook away the images. Sweet old grandfather types were too much to hope for in a shithole like this.

At least it was dominoes night tonight, so there would be another 10–15 bodies in at 8; it was only 7 pm now but she decided to take herself through the back to double-check the pies in the oven and that the rolls were all still there…mostly to avoid those coffin dodgers out front and check her phone for a bit. Three texts from Ryan: *"Did you see my CSCS card? Need it for that job that starts next week"*; *"Just ordered a big chinky, that's getting rattled then am havin a wank if you fancy sending some pics to help me out ;) ;) xxxxx"*; *"Teen, the CSCS card?"* She rolled her eyes and quickly let him know that said card was next to his passport in the junk drawer in the kitchen and she'd be sending him fuck all since the last 'naughty' picture she felt brave enough to send ended up in the 'Ibiza Beastie Boys' Whatsapp group chat but Ryan had honestly no idea how *that* happened. Luckily, it was just her tits and without anything remarkable about her body like a tattoo or a birthmark – he blagged it to his mates like it was some other daft cow. Not his own girlfriend.

With a couple of deep breaths and an adjustment of her top to make sure no cleavage was showing she shuffled back through to the bar. She gave the tables another clean and swept the floors beneath them for the third time this afternoon, even though no one had sat down there. At 7:50, she started pouring the Tennent's to save the swarm of thirsty middle-aged men nipping her head about not going fast enough if she couldn't pour ten pints at once. The thought of their possible passive aggressive remarks or jokes made her knuckles rigid and her jaw tense and she wanted to slide the pints down the bar to them watching all the glass and froth spill and burst over the bar creating madness and chaos. She didn't realise she looked like she was ready for a fight until Louis, one of the team captains, came in. His familiar aftershave breaking the stale guff of tobacco, lager and cleaning spray.

"Fuck's up wi you?" he asked.

Visibly pushing her shoulders down and releasing her jaw, she beamed a fake smile. "Knew you were coming in."

They both laughed. He asked if her dad was coming in tonight. How her mum was? How was college? How's the boyfriend? Usual pish and she complied with the normal, socially acceptable answers. 'Dad would probably be in later to make sure you're not cheating at doms again', 'Mum's OK, she's not back to work yet', 'College is interesting and Ryan is fine and doing away'.

Louis was always smiling. A really energetic, toothy grin that was hard not to smile back to and while he was easy to blether to, Teeny was sure his toothy grin would evaporate if he heard that his friend Alec would probably be in later if he hadn't already drunk himself to sleep because he was an alcoholic, albeit a social one. Alec's wife couldn't hold a conversation with anyone these days because the depression had gripped her so severely.

College was becoming unmanageable since moving into Ryan's mum and dad's house so they could save for their own flat. There was nowhere private to study, nowhere quiet to read and these late shifts in the pub made getting up for the early lectures fucking impossible. And Ryan? Well, he was fine and doing away; to add anything deeper would have alluded that there was something more interesting about him.

Teeny cringed at her cruel and aloof thoughts about her partner. After all, his parents' house was loud but it was alive. There was always music playing, doors opening and closing and playful arguing about what to watch on the TV. The routine of the frying pans clattering in the morning to the hum of the kettle boiling was soothing and welcome in comparison to her own parents' house which always seemed dimly lit, desperately sad and had a heavy darkness that clung like a hangover over it. The usual soundtrack to be heard was her father's unbearable drunken stupidity as he fumbled with keys, sang or swore to himself and any inanimate object in his path and the snoring that would vibrate the entire end terraced house. Or his seething fits of anger usually taken out on the poor inanimate objects when he was hungover.

On her 20th birthday, she had sat with her mother and father at the dinner table having tea and rich tea biscuits that were mostly stale. She worked up the courage to tell them that she would no longer be paying digs because she was going to move in with Ryan so they could save a deposit and buy their own place. She had planned to wait a couple of months to let them adjust and sort something else out financially. She was paying out most of her wages to cover the majority of the bills since her mother was not able to go back to work in the Co-op in her condition and her father was drinking every spare penny. Instead of the excitement and gushing she'd been showered with from Mags, Ryan's mother, her father flew into a rage, accidentally knocking the tea into her lap. Even as she hurried to the sink so grab a cold cloth to hold against her stomach, Alec continued to scream into her ear. "You selfish wee cow, look at your fucking mother, this will kill her!"

The swell of guilt rushed into Teeny's throat and she managed to choke out a "sorry" while looking at her mother who simply swept the broken pieces of biscuit into her hands and clapped out little piles onto the table. "Please yourself, everyone else does around here."

Ryan opened his parents' door wearing only his boxers, holding onto his cock like a pornstar assuming Teeny's 'I'm coming over right now' text meant she was coming to collect her birthday present earlier than planned. He quickly caught on that wasn't the case seeing her swollen red eyes from crying stained with make-up, clutching a shitty plastic bag with some clothes and a folder from college.

Now they were six months into their new living arrangement. Mags and Davie, Ryan, his little sister Joanne and Teeny. One big happy, loud, intrusive, chaotic family. Alec eventually had to make his peace with this if he still wanted to be served in his local and after a couple of months, worked his way up to asking his daughter directly to serve him a drink rather than simply putting his coins on the bar and wandering off to the bandit.

Louis wrapped up the small talk after waxing lyrical about his daughter graduating from Edinburgh University in the summer and how she'd be going off to Uganda to help teach English 'or some pish like that', he tailed off. He tried to downplay his daughter's success in the hope it allowed him to cling to his working-class roots but his fatherly pride was so clear and honest, there was no disguising it. He collected as many pints as he could carry back to the table and made sure everyone was ready and sitting in the right teams for the games to begin. There were a couple of new faces in tonight, one she vaguely recognised and the other she had never seen but knew he wasn't from here. Nor did he want to be. He held his jacket over his arms rather than put it 'round the back of the chair and looked as if the smell in the pub actually hurt the inside of his nose.

Prick, Teeny thought and watched him wander up to the bar scanning all the spirits with earnest. "What ye having?" Teeny asked.

"What gins do you have?"

Trying not to roll her eyes, she rhymed off the couple of house gins that were available and put together his drink and a Guinness for his friend she thought she knew who'd already sat down and was talking to Louis and Tommy.

"Sorry we're fresh out of lemon before you ask." She smirked as she slid the glass towards him with one finger.

"Christ, am I that obvious, like a spare prick at a wedding?" He laughed as he placed the note in her hand. "And one for yourself…?" He raised his eyebrows waiting for her name.

"Teeny," she finished.

"Oh, is that short for Christina?" he asked.

"No, like Teeny Bash. Just a nickname – everyone calls me it and it's just sort of stuck," she corrected.

"Like Baby in 'Dirty Dancing' you mean?" he pressed further.

She wasn't sure why, because it was a simple question, but she was becoming flustered and annoyed and felt on display.

"No, like Teeny. If it makes life easier for you to order drinks, my right name is Colette," she answered, pressing his change into his hand a little harder than she'd meant to. His skin was soft and warm and when her hand touched his, there was a little jolt that tickled all the way up her arm and into her belly.

He smiled back too sweetly. "OK, Baby. Sorry, Teeny. Thanks for the drink. I'd better go and take my seat."

He sat down beside Tommy and gave a brief nod of hello before talking to his friend and then beginning the game.

Teeny muted the TV then collected some of the pre-game glasses and put them in the washer before wiping down the bar. She allowed herself to stare at this strange man once the coffin dodgers had had a refill and were watching a muted re-run of 'Who wants to be a Millionaire?' He hadn't been overly tall and seemed slight in his stature. His silvery grey hair was quite deceiving as when he looked to the side and she caught his profile, he looked much younger. His strong jawline was framed with salt and pepper facial hair and she couldn't remember if he had blue eyes or green. She afforded herself a quick bathroom break knowing there were about five minutes before the first round of wounded shite players would be out and back up to the bar. She grabbed her handbag and found herself double-checking her armpits, reapplying deodorant and perfume and tidying her hair. She tucked her wayward bra strap back onto her shoulder and pulled her t-shirt down a little. She quickly glanced over her shoulder into the mirror to make sure she hadn't stepped onto toilet paper or had chewing gum stuck to her arse or something mortifying like that. She smoothed her hands over her breasts down her waist and over her hips and lingered there while looking at herself in the mirror.

"What are you doing, you tit?" She laughed under her breath and walked back out to the bar.

After another round of pints were poured, Teeny set about bringing the food out. Filled rolls and greasy pies that had been put in the oven hours ago before being heated up. How these guys survived a Monday night dominoes buffet, she didn't know. Unsurprisingly, *he* didn't eat anything.

Louis came up to the bar for a second pint and Teeny tried as subtly as possible. "So who are the new guys?"

"Who? Deek?" Louis answered nodding to his companion. "He works with me and Tommy down at the warehouse. Sound cunt, asked if he could come along for the doms since his local has shut down."

"And the other guy? The older looking one?" She tried for nonchalant.

"'Hink his name's Mark," he answered, spitting egg roll over the bar and attempting to wipe it with his sleeve. "He's Deek's wee neebor and I had said just bring folk along 'cause we were short on the numbers, he's awright but a bit quiet... 'Hinks he is somethin'." He gestured with his egg covered wrist under his chin.

Teeny nodded knowingly then went back to serving. She wasn't sure why but that made her heart sink a little. She thought about the jolt she felt when he touched her. Not that it should make a blind bit of difference to her but it did. She busied herself cleaning the trays and glasses waiting for him to finish. Willing for him to finish his game so he'd come back up to the bar. She pretended not to see him at first and stared intently at her magazine as he walked up with a few glasses then playfully peered down to catch her eyes.

"If it's not too much trouble, I'd like another drink," he said, still smiling.

She started to put the ice into the glass and tried to make small talk about the game but found herself stammering so decided just to stay silent for the rest of the transaction. She could feel her cheeks blushing and her hands shaking as she handed him his change. She wanted to hide away so absentmindedly pulled her hair forward to cover more of her face as she leaned over. "You should keep your hair back so everyone can see that face, be a shame to hide it away, Colette?" She immediately tucked her hair behind her ear. "Good girl," he praised. Then he was back at his table.

"What the fuck?" she found herself whispering aloud as she buried herself in reorganising the glasses on the bottom shelf so she could compose herself until the blood had drained away from her face. No one had called her Colette since high school, even college lecturers called her Teeny. A ridiculous image flashed in her head of her in a school uniform and Mark, the comical looking headmaster eager to discipline, donning a mortar board hat. She must have been more tired than she realised. She must have been downright fucking delirious at this point.

An hour later and the numbers were dwindling. Teeny had cleared the kitchen and mopped most of the floors leaving the two tables at the door where the final five were sitting. She'd already started to cash up and without realising, all the men were standing, putting their coats on and getting ready to leave. All of a sudden, she didn't want the shift to be over. She'd never see this guy again and couldn't very well go and ask for his number so felt a little crestfallen. Louis thanked her for setting up and gave a quick wave before heading out the door with the last few including the two newcomers. Mark looked back and gave her that same smile, wished her goodnight then just wandered off into the night.

She locked up quickly and walked home even faster, a strange, unfamiliar hunger in her. It wasn't particularly cold and she wasn't frightened, it was only ten minutes and she knew the route well. She wanted to be in a hot bath and then her bed. Attempting a bath or even a shower first thing before college was a non-starter since everyone would be fighting over the hot water.

She snuck in. It was only 11:30 but everyone would be long asleep. She ran the bath which was thankfully downstairs. She was grateful for the peace, the quiet and the privacy. She hadn't perfected the knack of the dodgy lock on the door yet and had already been caught red-handed shaving her bikini line at the sink by Ryan's 14-year-old sister Joanne. She still couldn't really look at her in the eye. She scooped her hair up high in a bun and didn't bother with candles or the light since it turned on the extractor fan. She lay there in the dark letting the water roll over her like a weighted blanket.

After a few minutes, she took the bar of soap and briskly washed under her arms and her back and breasts but then lingered over her knees and carefully drew down the line of her shins and under the arch of her foot pointing her leg high in the air. She pulled the soap back down her leg, down her thigh then rested it on the dish. She thought about Mark and his profile. His jawline and his chin. The sharp ironed lines in his black shirt. She played with her pubic hair and stroked her nipples while thinking about their exchanges at the bar. *Good girl.* She gently massaged herself and allowed the head tape to replay over again until her body became rigid and arched and then limp again in the water.

She could feel herself drifting to sleep so abruptly sat up and dried off before tiptoeing upstairs and climbing into Ryan's bed still wrapped in her damp bath towel. Shame and guilt swept over her as she leaned in to kiss his shoulder as he snored lightly. Her head felt light from the heat of the bath and the smell of the leftover curry sitting at the foot of the bed was nauseating. Time for sleep. She quickly set her alarm on her phone and pulled on a t-shirt and as she tucked the covers under her chin, continued to think about the man who'd made her feel so restless. There was a strong uneasiness in her gut that her head was trying to dampen, which made for a night of restless sleep and strange dreams.

2. 20 October 2018

She already knew in the taxi. She knew when he held her when saying their goodbyes that Mark would be furious. Her choices were to shun her friend and avoid contact and be scolded for being rude and standoffish or to casually embrace a friend and be accused of flirting and cheating later, at home. So, damned either way. She decided to hug her friend and take the shit later. Mark had dutifully held the taxi door for her, waved to Teeny's college friends and climbed in the other side. Teeny couldn't hear the radio, the other cars driving past or the crank of the hand break at every traffic light. All she heard was Mark's heavy controlled breathing and the soft scraping of his nails scratching away imaginary marks on his trousers. His steely eyes stared ahead. He didn't look at her and there was no casual chit chat with the driver who had immediately sensed the tone and focussed on the drop-off point.

As they pulled into the car park, Teeny's feet felt like cement in the car. Her knees were locked and her knuckles were tight. She didn't want to get out. Her stomach was at high tide and all the cocktails and shots she had consumed were sloshing back and forth, orchestrated by the nerves in her gut warning her about what was coming. As Mark paid the driver and came around to her side to let her out, she thought about quickly locking the doors, pleading with the driver to speed away and take her somewhere safe. To where though? Who would take her in? Who wouldn't tell Mark exactly where she was and the type of things she was accusing him of? So, she took his hand and climbed out and stood behind him with her head low as he fobbed his way into the building and then into his flat. Each door one step further into the maze, further from the real world and further from any chance of anyone seeing her to help her.

She had learned by now it was best just to let him say his piece, make his accusations, throw his insults and be quiet while he did so. Responding with reason and honesty only seemed to make him angrier. He walked down the hallway to the lounge where the kitchen was. It looked out onto the high street and the huge bay windows were fantastic to look out onto and watch the world go by. Did anyone ever look in? She took her coat off at a snail's pace and hung it up, carefully unstrapping each buckle on her sandals to prolong the inevitable. She could hear the ice hitting the glass and listened for which drink he'd pour. *Just one bottle. A heavy one. No mixer. Whisky. Fuck.*

She studied the coats hanging in the hallway which sat in an alcove with a huge standing mirror framed with an ornate wooden surround in it. She looked at herself, at the shadow version of herself she'd become and felt foolish standing there dressed up now in a low-cut dress which sat above her knees. He'd bought it. He'd asked her to wear it. She sidestepped into the bedroom to get changed into something comfier so she didn't feel so awkward wearing a 'slutty' dress when she could guarantee that's what she was about to be called. And she could run a lot easier if she needed to.

As she struggled with the zip, she could hear him summon her, "Colette. Where are you? Come here."

"Just in the room, two tics," she answered as she shuffled the black dress down to her feet and kicked it out of the way to never be worn again and unclipped the strapless bra. She sat on her knees in her underwear looking through the bottom drawer for an oversized t-shirt to wear to bed and as she reached for it, she could hear his shoes thundering through from the lounge. She tried to rise to her feet to explain that she was just coming but he already had her by the hair, his face twisted and furious. He gripped the hair just at the back of her neck and was yanking the handful upwards as if to use it like a dog's lead. It stung and nipped so much Teeny automatically obliged him by standing on her tip toes to relieve the strain and struggled to keep up with his movements as he pulled her into the hall displaying her up against the hallway mirror.

"Look at you, what do you see?"

Slightly dazed and feeling humiliated, she pleaded, "Mark, please, I'm naked. Let me get dressed and we can talk."

No sooner had the words left her mouth, Mark slammed her face into the mirror screaming "LOOK!" into her ear. Her eyebrow had split on the wooden frame and was now spilling blood down her face, mixing with the tears and mascara. Clearly not meaning to leave physical injuries that people would question, Mark composed himself, muttering, "This is what you wanted. You wanted all of this," as he walked back into the lounge.

Teeny turned away from the mirror and, falling to the floor cross-legged, silently sobbed into her knees still holding the t-shirt. She used it to stop the blood spilling any further since it was now trickling down her shoulder and chest and spotting over the floor.

After five minutes or so, the dizziness had subsided and she thought about getting up but could hear Mark coming back. This was it. Round 2. He was coming back for more. She tensed as he walked down the hallway towards her but instead, he turned left into the bathroom. She could hear the water running and him raking and shuffling through the mirrored cabinet. Teeny got onto her knees and checked the t-shirt, the bleeding had stopped. She feebly attempted to mop up the spots of her blood on the floor with the clean sleeve but only smeared it around the floor. She began to cry again. She just couldn't get it right. Mark heard her whimpers and came quickly out of the bathroom holding a small first aid box and a wet cloth.

"I'm sorry, sweetheart, I didn't mean to hurt you, I could never hurt you," he started as he came down to his knees and was gently patting the cloth against her forehead and eye to clean away the blood. "I only wanted to show you that when you dress like this, showing off your body, other guys will look at you and want you. You know that and I think you like it because you know it winds me up." He gently caressed the back of her neck as he pulled her closer to kiss the top of her head. She winced as her neck stung from having her hair pulled. He continued talking through muffled kisses into her hair, "Maybe this isn't what you really want, maybe you'd rather be out there with guys your own age and shagging about. Maybe that's what you need, not this life here with me."

Horrified and confused, Teeny found herself scrambling to try and get up and pleaded, almost whined, "No! That's not what I want, I want you, I want us! I don't want to be shagging about!" She stared at him wild-eyed and waited for his response as he stared at her injury, his lips a thin, tight line.

He finally exhaled a long-exaggerated breath through his nose. "Come on," he said. "I've run you a bath, let's get you cleaned up."

As he stood up, he offered his hand to Teeny to help her fully to her feet and took her elbow as she nearly swayed over back into the mirror. "I think you need to start watching how much you drink." He smirked. "You're falling about all over the place."

Teeny nodded and smiled weakly but knew any and all effects of the alcohol she had consumed had evaporated the minute she walked through the front door.

He guided her into the bathroom and helped her out of her underwear and step into the bath. She felt embarrassed and small. As if she was some drunken high school kid who had come and spewed everywhere and now had her daddy cleaning her up. He must have haphazardly thrown in some bubble bath before coming out to Teeny in the hall as the bubbles were frothy and high. This only made her feel and look smaller in the bath. She was grateful for them. She felt camouflaged by them and less displayed. She swept them up towards her breasts and neck and scooped her arms around her knees and let the warm water lap against her skin. The warmth of the water and the steam in the room enveloped her and the heat snaked into her sinuses, giving her a terrible headache. Her eye felt like it was pulsing. She half-winked, half-winced to try and assess how painful it actually was as she didn't want to put her hand up to it while he was watching her. After a couple of minutes standing over her, Mark lowered the toilet seat and sat down facing her, his fingers interlocked and he rhythmically massaged one palm with his other thumb.

As they sat in the uncomfortable silence, Teeny tried to piece together the evening. Had she been unconsciously flirting? Were any of her comments suggestive? Was wearing the dress a test? Should she have worn the jeans and top to pass this test? They had enjoyed a lovely dinner together drinking champagne and taking shots of tequila after the meal which had Teeny almost retching and Mark laughing at her clumsy immaturity when it came to taking a shot. He had insisted she pick a different cocktail in every bar they entered as well as leaving her purse in the flat.

"Can't I just have a Bacardi and cola?" Teeny jokingly whinged.

"No, it's a special occasion which deserves a special drink. Besides, we need to make sure this dress is well accessorised." So, there were photos. He had her pose with her cocktails in her tiny dress and strappy sandals.

"Stunning!" He beamed. He refused to get in the pictures himself, insisting she was the star of the show as it was her special night. They later sat in a quiet corner of the bar sharing the oversized cocktail, her sipping it and him sidled up beside her holding her hand and stroking her arm with his free hand, kissing her delicately on the shoulder.

"I'm sorry again about last week, that won't happen again. I'll work on my temper," he whispered. "I just can't believe you're mine sometimes. You know it though, right? That you're mine?" He had laughed slightly as he said it but it didn't reach his eyes which were boring into hers waiting for an answer.

She nervously played with the straw in her mouth and played with the cool condensation on the glass. "It's OK, I love you."

His eyebrows knitted together as if to question her response but the intensity of the conversation was pierced by a group of five or six people who burst into the bar with a contagious energy, laughing and joking as they gathered at the bar. One of them noticed Teeny and elbowed the small dark-haired girl next to him and gestured over to Teeny. She had hoped they wouldn't notice her. She didn't want to have to balance her two lives delicately and awkwardly.

"It's yersel!" The tall guy with a slick back James Dean haircut beamed as he and the dark-haired pixie broke off from the group to come towards their table. Ashley, the pixie, jokingly chided her friend, "Where the fuck have you been? I've been texting you to see if you had anything planned for tonight?"

'James Dean' broke her off. "Aye, I telt her you'd be staying in getting your end away and to leave you alone."

Teeny blushed at her friends' harmless joke. She was no prude but would now need to segue from that comment to "This is my b—my partner, Mark". She shyly introduced. "Mark, these are my mates from college, Ashley and Michael."

Mark smiled as he took their hands to shake and Teeny caught the judgemental side eye the two friends had given each other at her use of the word 'partner'. They stayed with her friends for an hour or so and the rest of their group all joined in too. They talked about college, the boring lectures, the assessments that were due in soon and all the stress that goes with it.

When Ashley and Teeny broke off to use the ladies, Teeny was reapplying lipstick while Ashley shouted over from the cubicle, "So, you're all loved up then?"

"Yep," she replied more curtly than necessary while blotting her lipstick. Ashley opened the door and hesitated as she reached for the hand soap.

"Are you…happy, aye? You seem a bit out of sorts and I know I gave you a hard time for not texting back but I'm worried about you, gal. You've barely been at college for at least three weeks and that's not your style."

Teeny tried for cool. "Well, maybe I'm trying a new style, re-evaluating my shit and deciding what actually makes me happy. Mark makes me happy and graded fucking assessments don't?" Her tone became quite clipped at the end.

Ashley quickly realised that now wasn't the time to have this type of conversation with her friend and she didn't want to piss her off on her birthday.

"Awright, chill out. I'm only saying 'cause I've missed having you around to copy!" She giggled. "Happy birthday Teeny, 21! Keys to the world and all that shite, eh? Right, I'm going to get some shots in, I hope you like tequila rose!"

Teeny forced a smile and tried to protest against any more shots but Ashley was already gone out into the bustle of the bar. Teeny stared at herself in the mirror. *Keys to the world.* She felt a little sad and disappointed but shook it off and quickly followed Ashley out so as to not leave Mark with a bunch of 20-year-old boys.

"He wants you, the big smarmy cunt." Mark intruded Teeny's thought process.

"Michael? I'm pretty sure he fancies Ashley, Mark, always has. He doesn't want me."

Guilt punched her in the chest as she remembered the cold winter afternoon when they had all gone to the pub after their last exam for the term. Michael had walked her to the bus stop, took her hands to warm them because she had forgotten her gloves and for a split second, she thought about leaning in to kiss him. He was so handsome and smelled so good but she broke herself away and they laughed awkwardly as she jumped on the bus and waved him off. She had never told Ryan, her boyfriend at the time, or felt particularly guilty about it as it had been a drunken moment of curiosity. A moment she had stopped. It had happened years before meeting Mark but she was sure he would drown her in the bath as she sat if she had told him. She was glad she was already red from crying and the warm water so he couldn't tell she was blushing.

"Don't be cute, Colette, did you shag him? No? Do you want to? You're just daft wee slags to guys like that. They keep girls like you and Ashley around so if they can't pull, they can just whisper sweet nothings in your ear and get a fucking leg over. Is that what you are? A daft wee slag?" As his voice boomed and echoed in the bathroom, Teeny winced and without thinking, put her hand up to her sore eye to feel the damage. Mark pushed his shoulders down, closed his eyes and took several deep breaths. Then he came down onto the bathmat and swept her hair back to take another look.

"I'll get some ice for the swelling." He left the room and Teeny peeled off her lashes since one was already stuck to her face using blood and mascara for glue. Then she carefully washed her make up off, choking her cries of pain into her arm. She didn't want him to feel guiltier for hurting her than he already did. Mark returned with the ice and held it against her eye while kissing her face then mouth, softly at first but then becoming more urgent and passionate.

Teeny couldn't match him and pulled away. "Mark, it hurts when I'm pressing into you."

Disappointed but controlled, he pulled back and then set about putting a plaster over the small split in her eyebrow. "Maybe you should stay home tomorrow, sack off your shift? I'll take us out for lunch and we'll have a nice day out?"

She'd had 'a nice day out' just last week when they ended up buying the fucking dress but she didn't want any unwanted questions about her face. She guessed that was Mark's reasoning too.

"Yeh, that sounds nice."

Almost relieved, he helped Teeny stand and wrapped her in a towel helping her to stand on the mat.

"Happy birthday, sweetheart." He smiled and kissed her forehead before heading back into the lounge to finish his drink, leaving Teeny to dry off and climb into bed. Her head was really thumping now so she opened the drawer hoping to find both ibuprofen and paracetamol. Just paracetamol. Without hesitating, she burst the blister pack, 1, 2, 3, 4.

Fuck it there's only five left and I need this headache to fuck off, I need to sleep, she thought. She rinsed them down with her glass of water from the night before and sunk into the oversized bed with the streetlight peering through and didn't remember seeing the minute change on the clock next to her.

3. 21 October 2018

She felt the cool breeze on her knee as it peered out from the side of the covers. Then fingers. Dancing 'round in circles on her skin. The groggy and heavy air on her muscles and head pinning her to the bed. Teeny wondered if she was still dreaming. She tried to focus and tune into her surroundings. She was awake but dreamily awake. She could hear the birds and traffic outside; she could smell bacon and coffee and taste the rancid poison of her mouth from forgetting to brush her teeth after a night of drinking. She could feel his hand on her knee. Already lying on her back, she kept her eyes closed and shifted her weight to expose more of her leg and thigh out from under the covers. He gently kissed her knee and reached further under the warm covers, skimming over her naked thigh and hips. Mark followed the trace of his hand with his mouth resting between Teeny's legs.

"Still asleep?" he whispered and she answered by flexing her hips towards him. "Thought so," he purred using his mouth and tongue to take away any pain and fear from the night before.

In that moment, there was no night before. She came quickly and hard as her eyes flitted open and her leg wrapped around his shoulders, tightening and pinning him closer to her. He pulled himself up, kissing her neck and attempting to kiss her lips. She shook her head pointing her mouth indicating that kissing was a no-go before she had brushed her teeth. He kissed her anyway, nibbling on her bottom lip as he moved inside her to reach his own climax. He crushed his face into hers, grunting and losing himself and as he did, Teeny remembered the pain in her eye, the tenderness on the back of her neck. She pulled her head to the side to relieve the pressure on her sore face. He lay there for a few minutes, afterwards running his nose up and down her neck.

"Am I forgiven then?" he asked.

"Mmm hmm," was all she managed.

He climbed off the bed and made his way into the bathroom next door to shower. Teeny sat up frozen, not wanting to move but needing to clean herself up and brush her teeth and get her hands around the coffee she could smell coming from the kitchen. She made her way into the en suite and thought about making herself sick just to shift the nausea she felt coming on but decided just to have something warm to eat and drink instead. She pulled on the white fluffy housecoat hanging on the door and scooped her hair up into a bun, wincing and gently stroking the back of her neck. She then peered at her eye which now looked puffy and a purplish-blue colour and the little white plaster was now matted with dried blood. She gently peeled it off and carefully used a cotton pad and cleanser to clean her face so she could avoid her eye. She rigorously brushed her teeth and tongue trying not to throw up. She walked through to the kitchen and could smell the bleach in the hall. Mark had mopped up the blood. She curiously checked the kitchen bin and sure as shit, there was her blood-soaked t-shirt. She'd had it since she was 17, it was her favourite night shirt but she didn't want him to feel guilty by bringing it out and trying to rescue it in the washing machine so she closed the lid and took a seat at the breakfast bar. Mark came through, his hair still slightly damp from the shower, wearing a white t-shirt and dark grey joggers. He always looked slightly strange when he was so dressed down, nothing like his usual smart casual attire.

"Good morning!" he said brightly and grinning as he walked around the other side of the breakfast bar to pour coffee for them both.

Teeny took the cup gratefully and started to spoon her usual two sugars into the cup when Mark raised his eyebrow.

"I thought you were dropping to one sugar?"

"I will, I just need it this morning to get me going," she offered.

"You don't want to get fat? In fact, maybe that's not a bad thing. Maybe no one else will want you and you'll be stuck with me. Maybe fire another sugar in."

He joked, she thought. It sent a cold chill down her back and she pulled the housecoat closer in as she cradled the cup to sip at it.

"You should have kept the ice on longer last night, it wouldn't have been as swollen. Do you still want to go out today?"

A loaded question. Was it her fault her eye looked as bad as it did now? Could she have made it look better? Teeny really didn't want to leave the house today. She didn't want to get dressed or wear make-up or have to consciously pull her hair over her face again so people wouldn't look or stare. It would be easier just to stay home.

"Nah, let's just stay here and chill out," she answered.

He seemed relieved. "Cool, if that's what you'd prefer. I'll text Darren from your phone to let him know you're not feeling well so not up to your shift. I can go and get us something in for dinner, you fancy a steak?"

Teeny nodded and smiled to feign appreciation. As Mark left the room to get dressed, Teeny reached for her phone to see what had been typed. There was no 'Hi, this is Mark, Teeny's not well' blah blah. No. This was a carefully constructed text that was exactly as she would have typed it. Her slang. Her emojis. It seemed harmless, her boyfriend texting in a sickie for her but something about it felt off.

Thankfully, Darren wrote back *"Nae bother wee yin, 'feel better' soon haha. Yer lucky it's no a Saturday shift. Hope you had a nice birthday"* peppered with laughing and spewing face emojis.

She looked through her texts and Facebook to see what it would look like to be looked at by someone else. By Mark. Was there anything untoward? Anything that could have her being accused of cheating or acting inappropriately? She checked through all the Facebook notifications she had missed from the day before, her 21st. Birthday wishes from school friends and Cross Keys regulars who would have no idea it was her birthday if Mark Zuckerberg hadn't reminded them. About two thirds down the notification list sat a 'read' notification from Ryan – *"Happy Birthday Teen xx".* She couldn't help but feel overwhelming sadness. She had broken his heart and flipped his world upside down yet here he was wishing her a happy birthday. She checked back to old photo albums on her profile. Feeling nostalgic, she looked for a specific picture of Ryan and her from their weekend in Aberdeen for his 19th birthday. It had been such a good weekend and Ryan, the stuntman, had nearly broken his arm attempting 'the worm' in the middle of the dancefloor trying to entertain and keep up with the locals. The photo was gone from her page. The entire album was gone. She scrolled further to find that several albums had been deleted in bulk. Any pictures with Ryan. *What the fuck?* she thought to herself.

It quickly occurred to her that this was no accident or glitch. This had been done on purpose, by Mark. This was the equivalent of her being pissed on to mark his territory. She was so angry. These were her memories. She didn't have them printed anywhere, this was her history, her life. It wasn't only Ryan in the pictures. There were pictures of Teeny singing with Claire, the karaoke legend in the Cross Keys. Pictures of the Colliers when she and Ryan were 18 and legally allowed into the pub to drink and even a rare picture of her mother smiling watching the men walk by in their black coats and blue sashes. She flexed her fingers with rage, her hands were shaking.

Before even thinking about the consequences of challenging Mark, she found herself screeching off of the bar stool and marching through to the bedroom clutching her phone.

"Who the fuck do you think you are?" she screamed at him holding up her phone.

Mark barely raised an eyebrow as he buckled on his watch and picked lint from his navy long-sleeved polo shirt he'd now changed into. "Firstly, who the fuck do *you* think you're talking to and secondly, what are you talking about?"

Teeny shook her head dramatically. "My photos, Mark, they're gone, all of them. Well, any that have Ryan in them, anyway. You fucking deleted them, why the fuck would you do that?"

Mark put his tongue to the corner of his mouth and held his chin as he exaggerated stretching it while pausing for thought.

"So that's your problem, darling. You're upset because all of your photos with your ex are missing? If you miss him so much, why you don't fuck off back to him?" His sarcastic and calm tone was unnerving.

Teeny regretted coming through to confront him already. Her rage was dissipating and fear was creeping in. "No, I don't want him back, I just, I just—"

"You just fucking what? Automatically assumed I'm some daft wee laddie who needs to delete your old photos to prove something?" he interrupted. "Don't take me for a fucking idiot, Colette. It's probably been an update or something that's deleted them but like I say, you can always go back and take new ones, get the real thing and not be here nipping my head about it!" He was shouting now.

"Mark, I'm sorry, I just assumed because they all happened to be with him in them and the way you've been acting recently…" she started to trail off.

He took two easy strides towards her and had her by the collar of the housecoat up against the door frame. He bit his lip to keep from shouting then spoke through gritted teeth, "The way I've been acting? Me? You're the one who's starting to act like a wee tart. Dressing like you're trying to get fucked out on the high street and turns out you've got all these mystery male pals that I know nothing about and then you still want to just come back here and play house with me?" He pulled her past him by the housecoat and tossed her to the floor like she wasn't even inside the garment. "I don't need this, I'm heading out."

He lifted his keys and his phone from the breakfast bar and stormed out the door, slamming every surface and door possible on the way out.

Teeny threw her phone with what was left of her anger and it hit with a satisfying crack against the radiator. She was angry at herself for picking the fight, angry for challenging him when they had just made up and angry for ruining their day. She crawled over to check her phone; she'd cracked the screen even worse than it looked before. Mark had grabbed it out of her hand the week before to check who she was texting and it hit the hard-tiled floor in the kitchen, smashing the corner and cracking the screen. She should buy a better cover for it, she thought. She tried to call Mark twice but it only went to his voicemail. Teeny cried in frustration then in pain from touching her still tender eye. She quickly showered and got dressed, hoping Mark would return and they could try and salvage their day and she could apologise for being stroppy and starting an argument. It was only just after 11 am now, they could still have a good day.

She took extra care to dry and straighten all her hair out, the way he liked it, and put some make up on. More than she normally would but she wanted to cover the bruising so he wouldn't be put off by it. An hour went by and then another. She phoned again. Voicemail. "Come home, please, I'm sorry," she left after the beep.

She didn't know what to do with herself. She cleaned the flat and emptied the bins so the t-shirt from last night was no longer there to see. She couldn't put the tv or music on as her nerves had her so on edge, she wanted to be able to hear if he was coming back. She sent a couple of texts: *"I love you and I'm sorry, please come back. I promise to be good?"* She added a heart and winking face to try and lighten the tone but felt embarrassed and silly doing so.

By 3 pm, she sat at the bay window with her legs stretched out along the pillows watching the rain, the people below scurrying into the nearby shops, bookies or pubs to get in from the cold, wet weather. She wanted to make it better. She thought about what Mark said and maybe she had been giving mixed signals about the type of life she wanted. He was her life now and if having friends that he didn't know upset him so much, she should stop contacting them. In a desperate attempt to show her loyalty, she opened Facebook then clicked the 'deactivate profile' button, deleted the app and then set about deleting some of the contacts from her phone. She barely knew some of them anyway. Some were contacts from the Cross Keys who would contact her for information about the darts or dominoes team and some were random people she was assigned to be in group projects with in college. She didn't need to have them on her phone. Delete.

She must have dosed off leaning into the window because when she heard the snib turn, she jolted awake to find it had stopped raining but was getting much darker. The clock on the wall told her it was now 6:30 pm. She pulled her legs 'round and tidied her hair and took a sip of the lemonade she had left sitting out earlier to try and wake up a bit. Mark walked slowly through the hall and hovered at the door of the kitchen and lounge. He left the lights off so his silhouette grew up the wall with his shadow.

"Hello." His voice was quiet and small when he spoke.

"Where have you been? I was worried – did you get my calls, my texts?" Teeny asked in a hurried, frantic tone that she couldn't calm.

"Yes, I got them but I wasn't ready to talk. You really hurt me."

Teeny walked towards him as he took a seat on one of the bar stools at the breakfast bar – had he been crying?

"I'm really sorry I accused you of deleting them and it doesn't matter, I don't need them or want him. I've deleted Facebook as well. Please don't leave me alone like that, please don't ignore me." she heard herself plead as her voice broke and she started to speak in a dry sob.

"What is it you want, Colette, what are we doing here? Am I wasting my time? You were the one who came crawling after me, remember?"

His words stung her, she remembered it as both of them being unable to stay away, both of them falling for each other despite the circumstances and the heartache caused to others. He was the one who kept showing up in 'that dive bar' as he described it just so he could watch her, or so he said.

"Well, I want to be with you. I want a life with you. I don't want to hurt you or make you unhappy?" she tried, feeling like she was attempting to pass a test with her words rather than make a declaration of what she wanted out of life.

Mark sat and thought purposely, taking in large breaths and releasing them at an achingly slow pace.

"I think you should show it then, be more committed to me, to us – if that's truly what you want."

"It is. I promise. I love you," Teeny said, still pleading then gingerly stepping closer until she was standing between Mark's legs and cupping his face. She kissed him quickly and pulled back still holding him and tasting the whisky that was now on her own lips. This made her stomach ache and sink. Her toes automatically curled in hard and tight so that she could leave her hands and fingers soft on his face. She had had no intentions of having sex. She only hoped they could rekindle so he would perhaps be sweet to her and talk to her calmly about anything else other than the last 24 hours. But now she could taste the whisky. He was drunk so could probably turn at any point. She didn't want him to be angry anymore, or leave again. So, she kissed him again, longer this time and more sensually.

She took his hand and led him through to the bedroom where they made love. Awkward, clumsy, drunk love. At one point, Mark had put his hands around her throat, not for the first time but it was the first time he had looked angry while doing so. Usually when they had experimented with rougher moves like this, they had felt consensual, fun and exciting, but something about his face tonight frightened her. She artfully moved his hands under her breasts to support her on top and she took her mind somewhere else until she could feel his hands tighten over her ribs and hear him call out her name. Teeny leaned down to kiss him and thought for a moment about mirroring his "Am I forgiven then?" from the morning but something in her soul wouldn't let her.

She moved off and into the toilet and waited until she could hear his soft snoring from the bed. She let out a long breath of relief then tiptoed into the lounge. She made some toast realising she hadn't eaten all day and sat with the TV on mute. She cried herself to sleep on the couch that night but couldn't think what specifically had bothered her or how to go about fixing it.

"What is it you want, Colette?" his words echoing in her dreams. Teeny realised for the first time that this is something she had never consciously done. Think about what she wanted. She slept with Craig Milton, the first boy to ask her to the Christmas ceilidh when she was 15, she then went out with Ryan for three years just because he asked her. She went to college because that's what her friend Nicole from high school was doing and she hated studying Accountancy. Hated it. She also ended up making her money working in a bar and spending most of her free time in it too. A bar where her own father had misspent most of her youth and continued to misspend most of his marriage. A bar where she felt a strange dull feeling in her stomach when it was too quiet, filled only with the coffin dodgers. She felt that choosing Mark, seeking him out and falling in love was the first thing she had had proper control and say in in her whole life. Now she wasn't as sure of herself. The look in Mark's eyes as he held her throat told her that.

4. 3 November 2018

Dinnertime on a Saturday night in the pub. Chaos. An unusual mix of the regulars crumpling up bookie slips and finishing their pints before their wives started calling or even turning up to collect them and the young team starting to come in for the warm up drinks before heading into town. It was karaoke night so it would be busy. These were the nights Teeny loved in the pub. She would be so busy behind the bar, serving almost became like a dance; swaying and side-stepping around Darren to keep the steady flow of serving going. No one would make small talk because they couldn't hear each other over the music and she would be in such a rush to serve the next customer she couldn't stop to chat.

Four hours into her shift, she took a break to get some fresh air. Fresh probably wasn't the best description given the thick cloud of cigarette and vape smoke that greeted her at the door.

"Be quick, don't take the piss, Teen…" Darren called after Teeny as she headed out with her juice.

She answered with her middle finger high in the air while holding on to her phone. They had been working together so long and she knew Darren much longer still, that their formal working relationship was sketchy at best. He would ask her to work an extra shift. She would tell him to 'Fuck off'. She would ask for help bringing the delivery in, he would answer by giving her the finger and tell her to hurry the fuck up. Never too deep, never too real. It worked well for Teeny. It suited her. She took a seat on the small stone wall outside and rolled the can over her chest, she was sweating. She cracked it open and took long slurpy mouthfuls, almost choking herself on the bubbles. She checked her phone. One text from Claire reminding her to check the extension cables for the karaoke machine before she came in at 7 to set up and six texts from Mark. A quick escalation from *"How's work?"* to *"Is it busy?"* to *"Don't be an ignorant bitch"*. Teeny sighed in frustration as she thought about how to reply. She started to type her apology and explain just how busy it had been when the football bus pulled in across the road and since Falkirk had won at home today, it was going to be a busy night for celebrating. Darren obviously spotting this too was wildly gesturing at Teeny to get in to return to serving the masses. Anxiety crept into her throat as she pushed her phone into her back pocket and one of the vapers held the door for her to head back into the fray.

The karaoke was in full swing and as was tradition, it was 'Tomboloke' night…a poorly named lucky dip karaoke where Claire would choose a theme for the first Saturday in a month and put names of songs into a hat. Those were the only available songs you could sing that night. If you didn't know the words? Tough. If you didn't know the song? Tough. The forfeit would be to buy the whole bar a round so more often than not, those taking the stage would warble their way through, leaving the rest of the bar in hysterics. It had been tradition as long as Teeny could remember. She had a fond memory of her mother, Denise, taking part. Teeny was only 16 and drinking lemonade, which her mother would top up with a shot of peach schnapps when no one was looking and Denise pulled Lulu's 'Shout' from the hat. She couldn't sing very well but everyone in the bar was shouting along with her, "Hey hey hey hey! (hey hey hey hey)!" Teeny watched her father stare in amazement at his wife who seemed to come alive and be free from the thick fog that was her own mind for at least this one night.

Tonight's theme was 'Saturday night at the movies'. Claire started the ball rolling with 'She's like the wind' and the atmosphere was high and the bar was packed. Like night and day from the dreary mid-month week days, the Saturday after payday in the Cross Keys was just the best. No high Vis jackets thrown over the stools while workers stood in their boiler suits and ASDA fleeces for a couple of pots before heading home. This was the night out. Couples came in arm in arm in ironed shirts and sparkling dresses. The dingy air was freshened with the aftershaves and perfumes and smell of hairspray from well-dressed men and women. It was a completely different bar. Teeny was glad she had worn a vest under her black shirt. She had wanted to wear her skirt too but Mark simply folded it back into the drawer and laid out her black jeans while she was showering. She didn't even think to argue about it.

She took off her shirt and tied it around her waist to get some relief from the building heat. She could feel her make-up sliding off with her sweat after going to great lengths to use extra concealer to cover up the bruising on her neck. This is what the shirt was for but she had supposed that it was darker now outside so shouldn't be as visible and everyone was well enough on, they wouldn't think to question it. The mark on her eyebrow had just about disappeared a few weeks on but had now been replaced with long streaked bruises just along her jawline and neck. Teeny noted that she no longer felt any pain when he grabbed her face to speak to her through gritted teeth but that it must have been sore to leave such markings on her skin.

She felt an extra sear of heat in her face each time she could feel the vibration in her back pocket when he was calling her but she couldn't answer as she wouldn't hear him and he would only get frustrated and shout to her to go outside but she couldn't because it was so busy. She'd already called in 'sick' too many times in the last month or so. She literally couldn't afford to get sacked. Not that she thought Darren would actually sack her but would more than likely give more and more shifts to Lynne who he already fancied, even though she was a hopeless barmaid. She didn't need to give him any more excuses.

In a brief glimpse of quiet, Teeny took the opportunity to go out to collect glasses. It was 9 pm now, she thought if she could fill the dishwasher and get a load on, she could get outside to call Mark before the load was done and everyone was ready for refills. Darren had been dicking around through the lounge having the odd trick shot on the pool table showing off with the young team under the guise of 'checking nobody was doing coke in the toilets'. She was due a break. She needed a rest and she needed to check in with Mark.

While walking past the karaoke table with an arm full of glasses, Claire announced, "And right on time, here's oor Teeny to take a shot. Roll up, kiddo…"

"No, Claire, it's too busy, I can't." Teeny tried to protest but Claire was adamant.

"Now, folks, it's a sad day when our own wee lass can't have her shot of tomboloke, I'm sure you could all wait three minutes to go to the bar 'til she's done eh?" She exaggerated a pouted lip at Teeny. "You know the rules, kiddo, tradition's tradition." She winked at Teeny off mic.

The bar cheered in support and Teeny knew there was no point in protesting further. Claire, with her perfectly bouncy hair and bright pink lips and blue eyeliner and low-cut sequined top which complimented her massive tits. She had an electric, persuasive personality and she always reminded Teeny of an old Hollywood type movie star.

"Fine, fuck it! Here…" Teeny gestured towards the hat quickly pulling the first paper she touched. 'Roxette – Must have been love' (Pretty Woman). She knew the song. She loved the movie and thought she would just hurry through it so she could get outside to use her phone. Having taken her singing talent from her mother, she screeched through the first couple of verses reaching the crescendo, "It must have been love, but it's over now, it was all that I wanted now I'm living without," and coughing and laughing her way through the rest of the song. She took her dramatic bow to the cheering crowd and handed Claire back the mic before picking the stack of glasses back up to make her way past the door to the other side of the bar.

Her heart almost stopped. The glasses almost fell to her feet. Mark standing just inside the door staring at her with seething rage holding his phone out. As she started towards him, he opened the door and walked straight out. No one else had even noticed he was there.

"Mon ti fuck, Teeny, I'm needing glasses here!" Darren roared from the other side of the bar.

She passed over what she had so far and stood trying to catch her breath.

"Chop chop hen, the table over there is full, hurry the fuck up!"

Teeny snapped back to reality and set about collecting the glasses. There were no further vibrations from her back pocket. By 10:30 pm, most of the more desirable crowd had moved on into town leaving behind a couple of the young guys who were barred from most of the bars in the town centre and two or three couples who were now entertaining themselves with the jukebox in the lounge now that Claire had packed up for the night.

Teeny tried to call Mark but it only rang out. She texted to say that she was sorry, she had been really busy and he should have stayed so she could explain. She asked him to come back. No replies. Around an hour later, Darren seemed to notice the change in Teeny's behaviour.

"You aright, wee yin? Did you lose your voice on the karaoke?"

"I'm OK," she lied, "just not feeling too clever."

He offered her an early finish which Teeny gladly accepted.

"Want me to phone that guy, Mark? To come pick you up? Don't be taking that walk into town, it'll be full eh fannys the night."

"No, no it's OK, I'll get a taxi, it's late," she replied too quickly.

She pulled her shirt back on and took another can of juice out to the wall to wait for her taxi. It had been unusually warm for November today but there was a strong, crisp wind now. Teeny was still sweating but it was no longer the heat from the bar. She was frightened to go home but terrified to leave it any longer than necessary. The buzz of the pub had kept her mind occupied all day and her inner thoughts quiet but now it was all she could hear. She could hear her own heartbeat whooshing in her ear, tightening in her chest. The blood felt like it was draining away from her face and flowing out of her finger tips and down past her knees. She leaned into her hands on her face to stop from falling all the way off the wall. She stared at the slabs in front of her, traced the lines on them with her eyes to try and regain control. She didn't know what was happening. She thought she was having a heart attack and before she could trace the full square, she saw the headlights of the taxi approaching. She climbed in and gave the address and put both hands on the seat by her sides to purposely feel the material and try to breathe. In a hard-northern Irish accent, her driver informed her it was a £60 fine if she was going to be sick.

"I'm OK, I promise," she lied again.

At the door entry, she clenched her fists and released them and then again. Then four more times. She knew this would be bad. He'd be angry that she didn't text back or answer the phone and then furious to see that she was singing of all things when he turned up. How could she explain this to him? She could tell from the car park that the lights were still on so he hadn't fallen asleep. He'd be waiting. He always did when she worked a late shift. At first, she thought this was sweet, he would pick her up if he hadn't been drinking or be waiting with a cup of tea for her and want to hear about her night.

Over time, this slowly morphed into a much more serious conversation or debriefing after every shift.

"Who was in tonight? Did they say anything to you? Did anyone ask for your number? Did anyone try and grab at you? Do you like it when they look at you?"

She found herself telling tiny white lies about who was in and who had spoken to her just to make her answers more palatable for him. Even though she wasn't interested in anyone else and Mark had been the only person she'd ever looked at twice in that place.

The first night he lifted his hands to her had been after one such late shift. She had finished her tea and was getting up to head towards the bedroom to put on pyjamas when he repeated his question, "Colette, you didn't answer me. Have you ever slept with Darren?"

She had thought it was a joke, that's why she hadn't answered. Darren lived at home with his parents despite being 37 and when he wasn't working, he was taking part in raids in World of Warcraft. He chewed with his mouth open, he smoked, he was totally sexist and above all else, he was Darren, Darren! The idea and imagery of sleeping with him made Teeny laugh, out loud.

"Naw ya dafty, he's Darren for fuck's sake, don't be so stupid!"

Already standing so close to her, he easily reached her with his full hand as he slapped it down hard over her face, knocking the cup out of Teeny's hand and the words out of her mouth. She had never been slapped before. She had only seen acts like this in soaps and movies. She didn't know what to do. She cradled her face with both hands as her cheek and head began to smart. She stepped back almost tripping into the breakfast bar but Mark was already over at her, scooping her into his arms.

"Sweetheart, I'm sorry, I didn't mean that. Please believe me I'm so, so sorry." He grabbed a dishcloth and wet it and held it against her face while using his other hand to stroke her hair.

When Teeny eventually found her voice again, she started, "I haven't slept with Darren. I don't want to and I never have. I've slept with three people my entire life; you, Ryan and a boy called Craig from high school. That's it. I don't sleep around," she finished.

"I'm so sorry, really I am. I just get so worked up sitting here thinking about all the attention you must be getting when I'm not there to protect you. It's because I love you so much," he answered. This startled her even more than the slap.

"You love me?" she asked.

"Of course, I do, I've never met anyone like you, Colette. You're fucking amazing and I sometimes can't believe you'd want someone like me and it hurts because of how much I've fallen in love with you. I'll never hurt you again though. Please believe me. Please, trust me."

She was crying now, as if the shock of the slap had frozen her tear ducts, his easy words had now defrosted them.

"I love you too, Mark, I do. You have to trust me too though. I've nothing to hide from you, I'm a good person. Even with Ryan…" She trailed off knowing Mark already knew she hadn't cheated on Ryan, other than with him.

"I know you are, I'm sorry. Come here."

She accepted his embrace and fell into his arms and let him soothe her with him stroking her hair and whispering, "I know you're one of the good ones, you're a good girl," into her ear.

Her hands trembled now as she got her set of keys looked out of her bag and fobbed her way into the building. She walked up the stairs to the first floor and opened the door which he'd left unlocked. She tiptoed through the hall keeping her boots on in case she needed to run, even though she never did.

"Mark?" she called out as she edged closer to the lounge. He was sitting on the sofa reading his phone with only the floor lamp lighting the entire lounge and kitchen open space. Teeny reached for the kitchen lights.

"Leave them off," he said.

"Why didn't you stay? Or answer your phone? I could have explained what happened, I really wasn't ignoring you, it was fucking heaving all day, honestly," she tried to explain.

"You must really take me for a fucking idiot. Do you know how it felt to be ignored all day by you when I know you're surrounded by other men who are drunk and leering at you? Do you know how it felt to turn up to see you to find you practically in your fucking underwear singing about how you were in love but now it's over?" he finished in a mocking soppy romantic tone.

"What? No! It's the fucking tomboloke thing, I didn't choose the song it's…"

Without being able to finish, Mark marched over to her, punching her with full force in her stomach, knocking her to the floor.

"Like that," he said coldly, "like a punch in the fucking gut."

Teeny's scrambled brain had taken away her ability to breathe. She sucked in air and struggled to get enough in to fill her lungs. She thought she was dying. She lay in the foetal position clutching her stomach as Mark paced around her.

"DON'T YOU EVER. MAKE A CUNT. OF ME. LIKE THAT. AGAIN!" The words punctuated with a hard kick to her stomach and legs and her arms inevitably from trying to shield herself. He smoothed back his hair and used the back of his hand to wipe the spittle that formed on his top lip.

Once composed, he walked back over to the couch to retrieve his phone and turned off the lamp and then walked through to the bedroom, closing the door behind him.

The song played over and over at full volume in her head. How could she have been so stupid? How bad did that look? She rubbed her shins and stomach and carefully sat up. She was able to quickly work out that she had spent more time on the floor crying in the short six months she and Mark had been together than in the whole three years she and Ryan were together. Was that what true love meant? To love someone this much meant this is how deeply you would feel about their actions or had Ryan not loved her as much as Mark did? Did Ryan just not care how she acted or conducted herself? She was so confused and hurt. And frightened and shocked. Moreover, she was exhausted.

The thought of this argument had been on her mind since 4 pm though she would never have imagined he would take it this far. She crawled over to the sofa and pulled the large throw cover over her. She didn't want to upset Mark further by attempting to come to bed. Each toss and turn on the sofa was agony. She tried her best to stifle her dry heaves and coughs as she moved, trying to ease the discomfort in her stomach. Sleep was impossible. At some point between 2 and 3 am, she rolled down her jeans and stroked over the welts on her thighs and shins that were already forming. Wincing as she stood up and pulled her jeans back on, she walked over to the kettle. She made herself a strong cup of tea and added a defiant extra sugar. She half-crept, half-limped through to the bedroom tiptoeing in and stood at the foot of the bed cradling her tea. He slept so peacefully. He lay on his front with his leg hitched up cuddling into the pillow she would normally lie on.

How could he sleep so easily, shouldn't he be racked with guilt and shame for hurting her like this? Rage swarmed in her stomach and her toes curled deep into the thick carpet. Her hands were starting to shake as she thought how easily she could throw the scalding liquid all over him and run before he had a chance to get to her. Teeny's menacing thoughts frightened her and she quickly made her way back into the lounge. She tipped the tea out and lifted the magnetic pen stuck to the fridge which kept memo notes like 'buy bread' or useful phone numbers for the local garage or window cleaner. She cleared a section in the middle and wrote GO FUCK YOURSELF before wiping it back off and writing 'I'm sorry'. She wasn't sure what her sorry really meant but figured it would cover all bases; 'sorry for not texting back today, sorry for singing, sorry it was a song about lost love, sorry I sweated so much I had to take my shirt off. Sorry that meant the bruises you gave me were on show. Sorry I keep disappointing you. Sorry I can't make you happy. Sorry, I can't take anymore'.

She tiptoed into the spare room where most of her clothes from Ryan's parents' house had been unpacked into drawers. Her day-to-day wardrobe that she picked from in the master bedroom had slowly morphed into a capsule wardrobe chosen and approved and paid for by Mark. She quickly stuffed some jeans, t-shirts and a couple of hoodies into her college rucksack along with her college folder and a handful of underwear. Her clothes still smelled like their house. Chip pan oil, cigarette smoke and black cherry Yankee candles which were Mags' favourite. Teeny wondered what would happen if she went there tonight, would they take her in? Would Mags put her arm around her and say, "Fuck him hen, you'll stay here and we'll look efter ye," the way she had done the year before when her own father had frightened and shamed her out of her family home? Highly doubtful. Margaret and David had made their feelings clear about Teeny after she broke their precious boy's heart. Loud and clear. In the middle of the pub; luckily, it was a Wednesday morning so it was quiet. Teeny, although filled with guilt and embarrassment, was still buoyed up with the energy and lust of her new relationship waiting at his flat for her. She would go home and cry to him and tell him about all the 'cows' and 'nasty bitches' she'd been called and he would kiss her and comfort her and assure her it was the right decision because he was the man she was supposed to be with. Not their son.

The memory of the heartache and disappointment in their eyes now made her feel so ashamed. She wiped her tears away and walked down the hall and into the common stairwell. The lighting in the landing was blinding compared to the darkness of the flat and she quickly made her way out into the night to somewhere safer. She just wasn't sure where that would be yet.

5. 7 April 2018

"Two Morgans and a can of diet coke," Louis ordered for him and his wife Sandra. "Eh…and a—DEEK, A GUINESS? GUINESS? Aye a Guinness for Deek, Teeny," he added to his order.

Sandra was looking really well. She hadn't been in for their usual date night on a Saturday in the pub for a few months. The chemo had knocked her for 6 and with her once bouncing curls gone, her confidence went with them. Tonight though, she wore a blue floral top with white linen trousers which complimented her new pixie cut wig. Between the new doo and the linen trousers, the signs were there; a new season, new beginnings. Spring had sprung. It had been as warm as a summer's day. The pub had been busy since the shutters went up with the new energy in the air and the sun shining. It had been unexpected since the early morning had been cooler and overcast.

Teeny had started her day frustrated and annoyed that she couldn't find any of her own clothes because Mags kept mixing her washing in with the rest of the family's. Teeny hated this. She purposely washed her clothes and sometimes some of Ryan's in a separate wash specifically so that she didn't need to worry about her boyfriend's mother handling her bras or shrinking her jumpers or telling her she 'maybe needed to buy herself new underwear because her pants were missing half the material needed to actually cover an arse'.

"She's only winding you up," Ryan would say to try and keep the peace which would only add fuel to her annoyance.

"Well, it's fucking worked; I'm fucking wound up!" she would retort.

Breathing his own sigh of frustration, Ryan pulled himself up off the bed from where he'd been watching Teeny slam drawers and throw piles of clothes around.

"What is it you're looking for, can I help?" he offered.

Teeny, finally finding her black and yellow tea dress she had been looking for, stood up.

"No, it's fine I've found it. It's to be nice later so I didn't want to wear my jeans and be roasting behind the bar. Just have a fucking word with your mum, Ryan, it's no' hard – 'Leave Teeny's clothes alone she'd prefer to do them herself'!" She dropped her towel and quickly pulled on her underwear and clipped on her bra, a race against time before one of them would barge in to ask if they noticed the sky was blue or something equally unnecessary.

As she scooped the dress over her head and sat down to lace up her black converse, she realised, not for the first time, that she was coming off as ungrateful bitch.

"Look, I'm sorry, it's fine. I'll speak to her – *nicely* about it tomorrow or something," she offered.

Ryan's shoulders dipped in relief, glad he didn't need to involve himself in the passive aggressive dispute about washing with his girlfriend and his mother. "You look cute in that, fancy a wee…" he started and raised his eyebrows suggestively.

"No," Teeny interrupted. "I don't. And I don't think you fancy getting to the point of no return when auld Mags comes in to offer a wee cuppa," she added playfully, sensing his disappointment.

"It's been ages, Teen," Ryan said sounding quiet and sad.

It had actually been about three or four weeks. She'd started to lose count herself. She'd managed to blame her monthly visit from Mother Nature for the first couple of weeks but he eventually clocked on that cycles don't last that long and hadn't for the last 3 years they'd been together.

"I'm just tired," she would say, or, "I think Joanne's still up." All valid excuses but nothing that had stopped them before. He'd often wake her up without any words just after his 6:30 alarm and they would make love as quickly and quietly as possible and she would giggle into the pillow as Ryan would greet his father on the landing – "Morning Da, beautiful fucking day eh" to a grouchy and half-awake Davie as they headed downstairs to make their piece before heading out to work. The truth was, her heart hadn't been in it for the last couple of months. She'd put it down to the pressure cooker that was their living situation, her complacency and apathy for her college work and maybe the fact that most times she saw Ryan these days, he was already in his bed asleep or sitting on his mother's couch still in his boxers playing with his phone waiting for his turn of the shower, his plaster covered clothes tossed carelessly aside. She was conscious that she picked unnecessary fights with him or worked unnecessarily longer in the bar or selfishly stayed later with Ashley and Michael in the pub next to the college to intentionally avoid him. He would text to tell her he'd be playing five a-sides then going to the pub and she would be relieved knowing she could come home from college, tell Mags and Davie she didn't want dinner and then lie in the dark room with the curtains closed and lights off at 6 pm just to breathe and only hear her own breath. Only feel her own pulse and not feel the strain of having to smile and chat or feign her feelings.

"It hasn't been that long," she corrected as she finished tying her trainers up. "I need to go, I'll be late." She chastely kissed him on the head and grabbed her phone, keys and headphones before slipping out the front door so she could avoid the bustle of the kitchen. She selected her usual walking playlist and allowed it to shuffle. Rilo Kiley's 'Silver lining' gave her walk a feel-good bounce to step to and she honed in on the lyrics 'And I've never felt so wicked, as when I willed our love to die'. Guilt slowed her pace and clouded her mind. She felt so out of herself recently, not sure how or why she was holding on to things, people and places in her life and it made her feel anxious. She was crossing the road to the Cross Keys now so tugged the earphones out and stuffed them in her jacket pocket, ready to step into character.

Deek. He'd been in that night with Mark. The strange aloof character that had been in playing dominoes a few weeks ago. Teeny felt an electric snap in her stomach when she saw Deek, wondering if he had come alone or had he brought his friend. She'd hoped so and secretly applauded herself for looking half decent for her shift for a change. She mostly wore a t-shirt and jeans to avoid any unwanted comments or 'compliments' from the old perverts but on a Saturday, there was normally two, sometimes three behind the bar so she felt relaxed enough to wear less of the armour.

Mark had floated in and out of Teeny's thoughts and daydreams over the past few weeks. She found herself fantasising about him while sitting in lectures and had willed his return to the dreary dominoes night the last couple of Mondays. She quickly poured the drinks for Louis and headed out to the other side of the bar to collect glasses. Also, she could get a better scan of the bar and lounge to see if Deek had indeed come alone. He had.

A couple of hours later, Teeny helped Claire set up the karaoke equipment and pass 'round slips and pens to the tables. She blethered with Sandra about how she was keeping and they talked about how her mum had been fairing recently. She made a point of making eye contact with Deek to ask, "You having a sing song tonight?" She went on to stutter her way through some small talk with him about his participation in the dominoes and enquired if he'd be interested in joining the team full-time. Luckily, Louis swept in to interrupt and steer the conversation to take the spotlight from Teeny.

"Aye, he's had a taste for a half decent team so he's coming for keeps." He laughed.

"And what about the other guy you brought the last time? Mark? We could always do with new players." Even Louis raised his eyebrow slightly, and subtly, but Teeny still caught it. Teeny could not have given a fuck about the dominoes team or the darts team and grudged having to feed them and put up with their demanding pish every week. So where was this team player enthusiasm coming from?

"Och naw, it's no really his scene man. He just came along to keep me company in case a made a cunt eh masel eh?" He laughed, gulping down the rest of his pint.

56

Deek rose to collect their empty glasses and make his way to the bar and added, "I said to him to come in the night though, for the banter likes. Said he might cause he enjoyed the company mare than the doms." He gave a knowing smile to Teeny that she couldn't quite understand but felt a tingle of excitement in her knees as she carried on walking through the lounge to hand out the rest of the karaoke slips.

The high spirits had put everyone in the mood to laugh, sing and enjoy each other's company. It was a rare night in the Cross Keys if someone didn't get put out for fighting, giving cheek to the bar staff or doing lines in the toilets. They would rarely get barred because they spent good money in there but Darren had to be seen to be taking some kind of stance against the blatant act. Tonight was one such rare night, when even the bar staff would take a turn on the karaoke or take time to chat out on the wall on their break without fear of an angry riot bubbling at the bar that required a squad inside at all times.

Teeny smiled affectionately at Claire as she started up her usual opening number on karaoke night – Black Velvet. The familiar guitar intro gave Teeny a small sense of relief or safety in the routine, she couldn't quite describe it but it made her smile and feel warm inside. Teeny mimed enthusiastically into an empty Bud bottle she was collecting as though she and Claire were having a duet from the karaoke corner to the other side of the bar heading into the lounge. As she weaved back through the crowds collecting the glasses and miming, she placed the glasses up onto the bar and playfully and seductively slid her back down the bar in time to Claire's "…if you please" and sashayed back up the way exaggerating swinging her hips and walked behind the bar. Only Claire noticed and laughed through her lyrics – all eyes had been on Claire and Teeny knew she could get a giggle. It was part of the fun to try and make her laugh while she was singing her heart out. A £20 note in her field of vision told her someone was looking to get served so she walked over and although she picked up the order perfectly; two Tennent's, a Smirnoff Ice, a vodka, a can of cola and a gin and tonic – she was completely stricken by the customer directly to the £20 note's left-hand side. Mark. She smiled politely to him and set about putting £20 note's order together. Once he had been served, she thought about the best thing to say. She wanted to come across as cool and gathered unlike the flustered girl he'd spoke to last time.

"What can I get you?" she settled for.

Mark paused as if not sure to say what he wanted and gave a small smile. "You're a really good dancer." He then gave a full smirk.

Shit, she blushed; he'd seen her. He'd seen her fannying about and dancing like a dafty.

"You saw?" she said, poorly concealing her embarrassment.

"I saw," he confirmed.

Teeny could feel the heat rising in her neck and resisted her urge to feel angry and ridiculous so she laughed and told them she'd got top marks for making a tit of herself at barmaid school. She sorted his drink and they made brief small talk before she had to move on to the next customer. He told her he lived in the town centre and drank in the Freebird bar before it closed where Deek previously played doms. Deek had convinced him to come along to keep him company and even though the Cross Keys was 'a bit of a dive', the scenery was nice.

"Nice to see you again, Colette was it?" The familiar sweet smile.

Teeny didn't think to correct him even though she never used her proper name, especially in here. She simply nodded and said, "Yeh, you too."

In the couple of weeks that followed, Teeny received more surprise visits from Mark and he came alone. She was unsure of the exact date but at some point, they had definitely crossed the invisible boundary into flirtatious territory. Her father would be at one end of the bar savouring his pint to avoid going home and Mark would be on a stool at the hatch where Teeny would return to in between serving. She didn't care who saw her. She was only talking. "That's it, lass, two wee bits eh ice." Rab nodded in encouragement as Teeny fixed his usual round. "And some cheese and onion crisps, doll." She leaned over stretching her arms which wouldn't reach the cheese and onion Darren had so carelessly stuffed at the back. She got onto her knees and took the other flavoured boxes down out of the way and leaned in to the back. Even under the counter she could hear Rab tell Mark that Teeny had "some erse" and what he'd do "if he was ten years younger".

More like if I was ten years younger, you auld creton, Teeny thought.

Rab and/or Stuarty's sleaze wasn't new but she felt more embarrassed and vulnerable tonight with Mark sitting there. Before she could say anything, Mark looked Rab right in the eye and with a warning glare told him that he would be better keeping his eyes on his pint. Rab quickly paid for the drinks without another word and sat down.

The coffin dodgers were quiet for the rest of the night. No one else had ever called those old bastards out. Not even her own dad. Her familiar shame crept up into her throat and around the bottom of her back when she remembered that she had been left alone in their company as a child in a room full of people and her one true protector, her father, had looked the other way. Intentionally or otherwise. She could never have a clear picture in her head of a memory. It was a feeling, a smell, a pain. She liked the way Mark's defensive glare made her feel. The way he made her feel. Important. Worth protecting. She smiled in appreciation and went out to clear the remaining glasses and start sweeping the floors and clean tables now that they were approaching last orders.

"Right, drink up folks, you too, Da." She nodded to Alec.

Alec, now beyond the art of conversation, muttered something incoherent and sank the dregs in his pint. "I'll shee ye-efter wee yin," he slurred to Teeny but looking quizzically at Mark who was studying his phone and didn't look particularly convincing that he was getting ready to leave.

When it was only Teeny and Mark left, she didn't want the night to end and ask him to leave but she did also need to go down to the cellar and cash up and lock up. They stared at each other unsure of who would make the first comment. She had explained who Ryan was as subtly as possible in conversation on previous visits to avoid being the 'I've got a boyfriend' girl too early on but also wanted to make clear with her words that she was spoken for, even if her body language told otherwise. Her smile when he would appear. Her dance-like walk she'd take around the bar to collect empties knowing he was watching her. Her heart pounding when she would

60

stand close enough at the hatch to smell him and hope he wouldn't notice.

"I suppose I better get cracking if I'm ever going to get to bed tonight," Teeny hinted.

"Does he wait up for you? The boyfriend?" Mark asked.

"Ryan? No, he's usually long sleeping before I get in. He keeps earlier hours than me," she explained feeling like she had to defend him.

"If you were mine, I'd wait up. I'd make sure I knew you were home safe in my bed so I could kiss you goodnight."

Teeny blushed deeply from her collarbones to the tips of hair. She felt a fire in her stomach that shook her and she felt truly speechless. She'd had plenty of punters in the past try to romance her and practice their best lines and she was always ready with a punch line or a witty retort. But this didn't feel like a line. His face was so honest, so unabashedly honest, it took the wind out of her.

He continued, "I can't stop thinking about you, Colette. I've never met anyone like you before. You're so much better than this dump and some guy who you never seem to see or doesn't even stay awake to make sure his girlfriend is safe after working with creeps like that all night." He gestured with his head towards where Rab and Stuarty had been sitting.

She agreed with Mark on that point. There had been times when she'd come home unable to sleep and cried about some of the comments that had been said to her and how they made her feel and that she felt unable to say anything back because they had been regulars for so long. Ryan would only laugh and say, "They're harmless auld bastards, Teen. Just ignore them."

She had never explained the strange mismatched memories that sometimes pulled her into a cloud of shame and disgust. She'd never been sure how to and didn't want to sound like a liar or a fucking idiot. She stopped telling Ryan about her experiences a while back. Unless there had been a full-scale riot in the pub with the police and broken glass, he wasn't interested. He drank in Morries, the bar on the other side of the cross. It had a better pool table apparently and a more desirable clientele than the spit and sawdust trademark of the Cross Keys.

"I don't think I'm imagining this between us, am I?" he interrupted her tangent thoughts. "I'm not just a sad middle-aged guy who's convinced himself someone like you could want me 'cause that would be mortifying."

In truth, Mark's age had never really occurred to Teeny. She found him so engaging and charming and handsome that she felt older than her years in his company. She had to have known these weeks of conversation and flirtation would build to this moment. She couldn't have assumed this desire would just burn away and she would serve his drink to him and walk away like she did everyone else.

"Mark, I'm…" she finally said breathlessly.

They had edged closer to each other during this time and he was only inches away. His tense breathing blowing the wayward wisp of hair that had fallen out of her ponytail. She could smell him. She cocked her chin up so that they were almost touching and when he licked his lips in anticipation, she could feel his tongue brush against her lip. Her train of thought disappeared. He kissed her so softly at first, she thought she had imagined it but his index finger brushing up alongside her jawbone centred her and she knew this was happening. She deepened the kiss and allowed her hands up onto his chest while he held her closer with one hand slipping down to the small of her back. She could feel his heart beating and taste the bitter juniper from the gin he had been drinking. Reality poisoned her tongue and the kiss tasted like ash as she pulled back, pushing his chest back as she did so.

"I'm…I'm not a cheat, Mark," she tried, attempting to get her breath back.

"So, don't be," he answered, smiling. "If you're not in love with him, leave him. Be with me. I think I could make you really happy," he said earnestly. So simple. Just like that.

She turned away to put some physical distance between them. Between her and the guilt she could feel swarming around her like angry wasps.

"You should go home, Mark. You need to go," she said, trying to convince herself that's what she wanted while unconsciously brushing her lips with her fingers touching where he had just been.

"OK, OK," he said still half smiling but with hands up like in a surrender. Continuing his playful 'don't shoot' stance, he went into his inside jacket pocket and took out a pen scrawling his number down on a half-ripped beermat.

"Think about it, Colette. Don't waste your life being unhappy with the wrong person."

Unhappy? Was she unhappy? Her mother had had clinical depression for the better part of ten years. Surely, she knew what unhappiness looked like? Teeny didn't spend her days crying or unable to get out of bed or listlessly staring out the window like her mum so she knew she was OK. Teeny would have her days where the world seemed too big to step out into but everyone had those days, she believed. Sometimes those days could last a couple of weeks or a month but she still made her work and still passed her exams. She wasn't an unhappy person. She realised that that maybe wasn't what Mark meant. Perhaps it wasn't so much the 'unhappy' part but the 'wasting' part. She too had sensed she was going through the motions of her relationship but had never thought to stop the burrowing long enough to look up and see if she was actually going in the direction she wanted.

Mark slid the beermat along the bar and as he walked towards the door, stood shoulder to shoulder with her, Teeny facing the large mirror on the wall and him facing the door. He ran his finger down from her shoulder to her elbow and back up.

"Think about what you want," he said once more then walked out under the half-pulled shutter and then pulled it all the way to the floor for her. Teeny, realising she had been holding her breath since he last used her name gasped out and tried to catch some air holding her mouth and her stomach. She quickly followed where Mark had left and locked the shutter. Unsure she could stop herself if he decided to come back under the shutter. She paced the floor then eventually sat on the leather booth seat. To ground herself, she ran her hands over the leather, feeling the cool material under her palms and listening to the gliding sound they made. She could still smell him. Taste his gin on her lips. She laughed manically at herself and the ridiculous situation she found herself in. Put herself in. Then as she made her way to the cellar to cash up, she realised she would eventually need to go home to Ryan tonight, climb into his bed, in his parents' house and sleep knowing she had betrayed him and couldn't promise herself she wouldn't again.

6. 4 November 2018

The thrashing of the delivery being emptied from the lorry and the piercing curses of the driver to the Co-op staff startled Teeny awake. Her cheek damp from the pool of saliva that had formed on the leather seat. Her neck was stiff and she carefully lowered her feet off of the wooden chair she had used as an extension of her makeshift bed. She could hear the low hum of the refrigerators and the dishwasher. She had eventually fallen asleep around 5 am and her rude awakening told her it was daytime, somewhere between eight to nine when the Co-op delivery would come in.

She lay there for a few minutes. Her phone had run out of battery around 4:30 am after she spent the time reading and re-reading text messages to piece together how she had come to this point. Was she a good girlfriend? Was she as loyal and faithful to Mark as she imagined herself or had she now fully embodied this new persona of being a horrible slag who broke hearts and led men on? She would need to sit fully up to be able to see the clock on the wall. 8:45 am. It was a Sunday so Lynne who normally picked up the cleaning shifts wouldn't be in until ten today. Teeny took another swig of the cola she'd helped herself to and tried to sit all the way up, holding her body together as though she might fall apart on the way up. She felt bruised all over. She took her rucksack into the toilet and tried to clean herself up. She took some toilet roll and wet it to try to clean off the smeared make up underneath her eyes and put on some deodorant and changed her t-shirt. She put a pound in the machine to get herself a chewable toothbrush and attempted to freshen her breath. In her haste, she hadn't lifted her phone charger or dry shampoo so her hair would need to be scooped up using a rubber band to keep it tied up.

Fear crept up her back in a sweat. She worried about how Mark would react when he woke up and she wasn't there. When he read her note on the fridge. When he would try to call her and get put straight to her voicemail. A tiny tingling of excitement that he might be really worried about her and be overcome with guilt and try to find her also beaded on her skin but she was mostly afraid. She felt out of control. She packed up her bag and carried out a quick clean to clear the scene as if she hadn't snuck into the Cross Keys at 3:30am to sleep like an auld jakey. She stepped out into the bitingly cold morning and stuffing her hands into her pockets, made her way up the hill to her own parents' house.

She stopped at the shop to pick up some rolls, sausage and milk in the hope it would distract them from wondering why their estranged daughter had shown up suddenly, unannounced and so early on a Sunday. Alec was still asleep when Teeny came in the back door, which was always unlocked but there sat Denise cradling her cup of tea, watching the tiles on the walls as though they may change shape if she looked away too soon.

"Morning, Mum," Teeny said softly as she came in, trying not to frighten her out of her trance.

"Oh, hiya doll. It's good to see you. I was just saying to your dad yesterday I need to come down to the pub so I can see ma wee Teeny."

Denise was slowly stretching herself off of her seat to make her daughter a hot drink but hadn't expected Teeny to throw herself into her mother's arms. Teeny felt so overwhelmed. With guilt for rarely visiting her mother. With sadness for her mother's poor mental health. With sadness for herself. She heaved great loud sobs into her mother's chest muffled by her lilac fluffy housecoat she had had for years. Teeny bought it for her mother's Christmas when she was nine. She remembered proudly wrapping it herself after spending her very own pocket money buying her a gift for the first time. She breathed her in; Nivea moisturising cream, rich tea biscuits and a sweet indescribable scent that could only be noted as 'Mum smell'.

"Oh Mum, I'm sorry," was all Teeny could get out in between her sobs, which made her chest hurt and her stomach even more so.

"What's all this, wee yin?" a wild-eyed Denise asked as she stroked her daughter's greasy hair. "You're alright, darling, you're alright. C'mon let's get the kettle on," she said as she patted Teeny's arms, signalling she'd had enough of this intimacy and she was too close.

Teeny sniffed and caught her breath remembering where she was and that her mother couldn't hold her like that, she could barely hold herself.

When the two women had their cups of tea, they sat in silence for a few minutes.

"I just missed you guys," Teeny lied. "The guys in the pub were asking how you were last night and I couldn't give them an honest answer because I've not seen you for about six weeks and I'm really sorry about that."

In truth, Teeny did feel more guilty anytime someone would ask how her mother was as she had seen her less and less since moving into Mark's flat. It had been unintentional but she had just kind of…fallen away.

Her mother looked at her suspiciously and sipped her tea.

"And you needed to get up with the birds and come and see me in my jammies without even having a shower because you missed me so much?" She scoffed a little.

Teeny knew it was a transparent excuse but she didn't want to tell the truth. A part of her already knew she would somehow end up back with Mark and didn't want to give herself the additional emotional admin of having to 'untell' people that he wasn't quite the Prince Charming she had sold to them.

Teeny cooked off the sausage as Denise went to shower and as if the smell wafting upstairs acted as some kind of alarm, Alec appeared in the kitchen. Teeny knew the routine; two paracetamol and a glass of Irn Bru before any kind of chit chat. This morning, despite the unusual visit, was no different. As he let out a huge belch after gulping half of the glass he asked if any of the sausage was for him. Teeny was grateful that her father was strictly useless when it came to her welfare as he hadn't seemed to pick up on her tear-stained face or dishevelled appearance. That being said, he saw her the day before in the pub, he'd been in watching the horses with Rab and Stuarty. To him, there seemed to be little difference between seeing his daughter behind the bar serving pints and serving him a roll-on sausage in his own kitchen when she hadn't lived there in over a year.

After they'd eaten in silence, Alec slowly shuffled off to the living room to plan his day's viewing based on which game played when and which time which horses ran. The familiar crack of the Tennent's at 11 am told Teeny her father wouldn't be much company from here on out.

It was still so bitter and frosty outside, as if there had been the lightest powdering of snow. Teeny and her mother sat in the kitchen and as she looked out of the window while cleaning the breakfast plates, she lost herself in the winter wonderland of the garden. The sparkling beaded crystals on the washing line, the overgrown grass feathered white with frost and the remaining leaves that hadn't blown away were now glued to the ground, frozen in time, as if winter had come so suddenly the clocks forgot to keep up.

"So, when do I get to meet the new man?" her mother asked, breaking Teeny's train of thought and emphasising on 'man' or so Teeny heard.

"Soon, Mum. He's just busy at work a lot and then I'm the pub all weekend most the time, it's hard to get a good time."

Her mother asked more questions about the mystery man that had apparently swept her daughter off her feet and scooped her away from the small village, for most of the week anyway, when she wasn't working in that shithole down the road. Denise had secretly been proud but managed to keep a straight face when Alec would drunkenly rant about that 'aulder fella' that was 'hingin aroon Teeny like a flea roon shite'. Her mother had always liked Ryan, he was a nice boy but she could see her own life replaying in colour right before her eyes. First boyfriend out of high school, all loved up, moving in together, never leaving the village, never looking for a career beyond the Cross. She had been happy in her young years dancing around the memorial at the Cross with Alec. Dancing to imaginary music only they could hear and singing as they shuffled home, drunk on wine and each other, to their little end terrace to let the babysitter away and peek in at her precious girl sleeping. It was a small, comfortable but happy life. She'd wanted more children. A boy. A playmate for Teeny Bash. They'd tried for years without any luck which confused both of them as she had got pregnant so quickly with Colette, without trying, without meaning to and without being married first. A quick trip to the registry office soon meant they could enjoy their little family of three. As the years of an absent cot grew on so did her disdain for her husband.

Maybe if he stopped drinking, he could get it up, she thought. *Maybe if he stopped drinking, his swimmers wouldn't be poison. Maybe if he stopped drinking, I could stand the sight of him.*

Finally, when Teeny was around ten, by luck or by chance, she fell pregnant. Unfortunately, the little girl was never meant to meet her big sister and because she'd only been 19 weeks when she miscarried, they simply took her away, like a faulty appendix. Denise would have named her Susan. Her pain and heartache anchored deep in her chest and it never really lifted. She felt guilt any time she looked at Teeny for failing to give her a sibling and hatred anytime she looked at Alec for only tuning into his own needs when her soul was crying out to be held and looked after and comforted. He abandoned her, painfully slowly and selfishly. She didn't want this life for her daughter. She wanted Teeny to cast her net wider and run and jump into adventure, see new people and do new things. She heard about the older guy and thought to herself, he'll not be interested in having kids surely at his time of life. He'll take her away from this god-awful place and she can really make something of herself.

Teeny told her mother how Mark worked for a head-hunter organisation meaning he sought people out and put them in better employment/positions that were more suitable. She realised the irony in this while explaining to her mother, that that was essentially what he had done with her. Headhunted her. The memories of his first few appearances in the pub made her smile. She went on to describe his beautiful flat and the outlook and what the neighbourhood was like but deliberately failed to mention what he was like with her. Was he kind? Did he make her laugh? She thought it best to stick to the safer topics. She couldn't trust herself not to start sobbing again. Her mother, weary from all this conversation that she simply was not used to, excused herself and went upstairs to have a sleep. Teeny found herself rattling and the adrenaline of keeping face to her mother was wearing off, she helped herself to her dad's paracetamol.

I'll just take four, she thought. *Just to last longer.*

She wandered up to her old bedroom and though her bed had been sold or given away, most of the room still looked the same, just a little dustier. She looked through some old photo albums and cringed at a couple of old diary excerpts and then picked up her copy of *The Catcher in the Rye*. She should have returned it at the end of the school year back then but fucking hated Mr Dixon so kept his book. She didn't really understand the story at the time and realised she hadn't really tried, to spite her teacher. She read a few pages and was instantly gripped. Reading for an hour or so before sleep weighed heavy on her eyelids and she pulled out an old sleeping bag that she remembered was in her wardrobe and pulled it over her and lay on the floor. She breathed in the familiar yet strange smell of home and drifted off to sleep.

"You still here, wee yin?" her father's voice boomed and he flicked on the bedroom light since it had got dark outside.

Teeny's defensive hand flew up as if to stop the pain of the light in her eyes.

"Aye, sorry Dad. I fell asleep. Can I just kip here tonight, I'm not feeling great."

"Aye, 'course ye kin, pet," he said.

It must have been a successful day on his betting slips. His spirits were high and he didn't question her fake illness or if she needed medical attention or if maybe he should let her partner know where she was and that she was staying over.

She could hear and smell her mother making mince and tatties. Her favourite. She hadn't eaten it for months as Mark viewed it as a 'pauper's dinner'. She peeked her head into the kitchen to ask if her mum needed any help and noted her father had already fucked off to the Cross Keys. He'd be eating his dinner cold at around 10 pm tonight. Teeny looked in her hurriedly packed bag and laid out some clean clothes. She felt sticky and sweaty and uncomfortable from all the half-attempted sleeps and rests she'd had in the last 24 hours. She went into the bathroom and opened the window wide remembering the extractor fan didn't work and the patch in the corner of the ceiling would get all black again if it didn't get aired out properly. She showered and turned the heat all the way up to somehow treat her skin and renew it. She used her father's Tesco hair and body gel to wash herself as she didn't want to use her mother's good, expensive stuff. She knew it was important to her and her only real luxury she afforded herself.

She stepped out onto the mat and watched the cool winter air shift the billows of steam off her skin and swoop them out into the cold evening. She brushed out her hair and let it dry by itself into their natural wavy state. She felt clean but had forgotten the pain on her legs as she roughly dried them. She ran her hand down her legs to assess them. Large welting blueish bruises. They looked worse than they felt and Teeny was conscious that they would only get worse looking as the days would come. She pulled on some old pyjamas she had luckily left behind in the set of drawers and big oversized slipper socks. She felt so young and small and wanted to lean into it and enjoy this feeling, feel like she was being looked after and loved and wearing fluffy slipper socks.

As she walked down the stairs, her mother was plating up and they took their dinners onto their lap and watched the television. She savoured the meal, mopping up the gravy with the buttered bread. Even when she would have this at Ryan's, it was never as good as when her own mother would make it. She licked the buttery gravy as it ran down her hand and caught her mother looking at her fondly. Nostalgically.

"You did always like yer mince and tatties, wee yin." She laughed as she went back to her own meal picking out the onion.

"Why do you do that, Mum? Why cook it with onion when you hate it and you need to sit and pick it all out?" Teeny asked.

Her mother thought about her answer as if she hadn't ever really asked herself that question. "Eh…your dad liked the

73

onion and you ate it with onion so I just always put it in then pick it out and got used to the flavour."

Teeny nodded to signal she understood the explanation when actually there seemed to be at least five alternatives to this set up that she thought of straight away but then she realised that maybe her mother just couldn't bring herself to break away from the routine, of even the smallest of things.

Teeny cleaned the dishes as her mother caught up on the 'X-Factor' she had missed the night before because her father had come in at teatime, drunk, and snored so loudly and obnoxiously it wasn't worth sitting trying to listen to the show through it.

Teeny wondered where Mark would be at this very moment. Would he be roaming the streets looking for her, asking around in the Cross Keys, would he speak to her dad? The thought filled her with dread. Mark didn't know where her parents lived. She'd never brought him to visit yet. Surely, he wouldn't tell her father why he couldn't find her himself? Would he phone the police or hospitals, paranoid that maybe she'd had internal bleeding after that punch? The thoughts swam through her brain and she suddenly felt so guilty for leaving him. For leaving him to wonder what had happened to her. It was so thoughtless and selfish. She should have stayed to talk it out in the morning when his temper had calmed down. Her throat felt tense and her jaw tight as she tried to fight tears. She could hear the ad break so her mother would probably be through any minute.

They sat together on the sofa channel surfing for a bit before settling on the movie 'Goodfellas' which had started half an hour or so ago. They'd both seen it before so could pick it up pretty easily and let it wave over them while they both sat equally distracted by their own minds not paying any particular attention to the television at all.

"Right, I'm heading to bed before that gibbering idiot gets in," Denise said as she shuffled out of the room waving goodnight to her daughter. Teeny turned the TV off so she could hear her father coming. Just like clockwork on a Sunday, 10:03 pm. She heard the singing first then the keys hit the doorstep. Then the cursing. "Get yersel ti fuck, you fuckin' wee bass, there ye are."

She skirted 'round the sitting room and dived up the stairs to the landing so she could hear him come in but let him assume she was already in bed. She could hear him meander down the hall towards the kitchen and peel back the tin foil to his dinner. She could hear him slop over the meal like a dog from up the stairs but was satisfied that he was alone so left him to it and tiptoed in to her room for the night. She left the blinds open so she could look at the clear sky and the twinkling stars. They were beautiful. She tried to suffocate the panic she could sense when she pictured Mark's face. When he read the fridge note. When he phoned her mobile. She couldn't hide here forever. She would need to speak to someone or say something. She continued to lay in the dark sweating until exhaustion took over and granted some relief.

Her father, despite being an alcoholic, did always seem to manage his work. This had always impressed Teeny and probably helped disguised his alcoholism until she herself was the barmaid enabling him. He would finish around 2 pm and then the van would drop him off at the Cross so he could top up his reserves before coming home closer to 4 pm.

It was nearly 11 am, Monday, and Teeny should be in a tutorial class in 20 minutes' time but she had no intention of going. She had stopped opening the emails and letters about her attendance and grade average going down. She really should go in and speak to student services but not today. She woke up and dozed between 6 am when she heard Alec wandering around and getting ready for work until around 10:30 am. Her face felt swollen with sleep. She peeked over at the mirrored wardrobe and saw her puffy lips and eyelids and her wavy hair, a tangled mass at the back of her head. She shook it free in an attempt to loosen it up and tousle it down so she wouldn't need to wash it again today. She quickly showered to wash off the dust and sweat from lying on the floor under a sleeping bag all night and got dressed back into her jeans and one of the oversized hoodies. She had tea and toast in the kitchen with her mother who sat in silence looking at her own phone playing candy crush or something Teeny guessed.

"I'll just pack up a few more of my bits from upstairs then I'll head back into town," Teeny offered as way of explanation that she wasn't ready to go home yet. Her mother simply nodded. Perhaps too exhausted from exerting herself into socialising with Teeny the day before. Teeny didn't take it personally. It was the most time and conversation she had had with her mother in so long. She excused herself and went back upstairs and folded up the sleeping bag to use as a seat.

She studied the fragments of her memories more carefully this time. Mixed CDs she'd burned to listen to on repeat, friendship bracelets, birthday cards. Little pieces of herself she hadn't the heart to throw away but also not take with her for her journey into adulthood. She picked the novel back up and continued to read *The Catcher in the Rye*, conscious of her mother's odd trip to the toilet or in her own room changing the washing on the clothes horse but confident she wouldn't come in to check on her. She was entranced in the story. She teared up reading Holden's final words: *"It's such a stupid question, in my opinion. I mean how do you know what you're going to do till you do it? The answer is, you don't. I think I am, but how do I know? I swear it's a stupid question."*

She loved Mark. She realised the pain she was feeling wasn't only her bruised leg and sore stomach. She missed him. She felt as if part of her were missing. Like a fly with its wings ripped off. But this wasn't normal. His reactions and treatment of her were not normal and were steadily getting worse. She knew that and deep down had known it was building for weeks. What should she do? What could she do? She held the closed book up to her chest and noted it was already getting darker and she could hear her father's voice talking as he made his way off the street into the front garden.

Fear and excitement shot up her back and neck and she was on her feet. He wasn't alone. She tried to steady her breath as she walked down the first few stairs so she didn't sound like she had just been running.

"Look wha' a foond!" her father proudly proclaimed, showing off his trophy. Mark. In her parent's hallway.

"Hello, sweetheart," he greeted her. "I've missed you," he added biting his bottom lip a little. He was testing the waters; had she told them, told her mother?

"I've missed you too," she responded meekly and without hesitating walked right down the stairs and into his embrace to give him a short sweet kiss, still conscious her father was within a metre of her.

Alec rolled his eyes and walked off towards the kitchen taking his high viz off and peeling off his boiler suit, explaining to Denise who was here and to get the kettle on and more Tennent's into the fridge. Teeny and Mark stared at each other and to break the tension, she reached up and kissed him again, holding his face and drinking him in. She could feel his shoulders relax and almost hear him sigh in relief as they kissed. Aware her parents would be back in the hallway at any moment, she pulled back a little and they rested their foreheads against each other and he held her chin with both hands' thumbs, stroking her lips. *Holden was right,* she thought, *it was a stupid question.*

7. 2 May 2018

'Message sent'. Her hands sweating as she tapped the screen. Mark hadn't returned since the night they had kissed. He'd very much left the ball in her court since he'd left her his number but didn't have hers and had stopped popping in. Two weeks had passed. The shifts dragged in. She found she was edgy and intolerant of the punters and sat with a face like a smacked arse most of the night. Eager to lock up and just go home. She'd even brought down her college books to start making some notes for her assessment knowing there would be less than a handful in and no decent conversation. She might as well study.

"Are you avoiding me?" She signed off the text with 'Teeny' before correcting it to 'Colette'. 45 minutes had passed and she must have checked her phone for 36 of those at least.

"No. Just didn't want to pester you? You're the one who sent me home?" he finally replied.

She quickly scanned the text then had to serve. She quickly threw the drinks together to get back to her phone which was charging at the hatch. A follow-up message from him.

"Have you thought about what you want?"

Teeny had wanted to point out that it was unfair of him to just declare his feelings, for them to kiss once and with no follow-up conversation and then for him to expect her to have a readied response. She started to type out *"You"* and accidentally hit send too soon. She frantically started to write out the correction and not just leave it as open and blatant but then hesitated. It was a little cliché but maybe it was the Freudian slip she needed. The 'sign' she had been waiting for to help guide her thoughts and what she wanted to do. She decided to let the chips fall where they may and see what he would reply.

She fidgeted and read and reread pages in her book. Highlighting words she hadn't taken in and switched her phone to silent so she needn't torture herself further. She took the spirit bottles down from the shelf and cleaned them to kill the time. She swept the floor and cleaned the pictures and mirrors on the wall to keep away from the hatch when no one was needing served.

"Fuck sake, the queen comin' in for a hof hen?" her father commented when he came to order his drink.

"Just passing time," she replied.

She even indulged the coffin dodgers by helping them answer a couple of questions on 'who wants to be a millionaire' since their music knowledge would have used every one of their lifelines. 10:30 pm and most of the bar was empty other than auld Tam who still had a full drink and the coffin dodgers who had been nursing their pints for the last 20 minutes or so, getting ready to see who would take the last hit at the bar. Still no reply.

She did, however, receive four texts from Ashley quoting varying parts of the textbook with the caption… *"We're meant to know this? WTF?! :/.*" Teeny smiled through her frustration and put her phone back.

She headed through to the kitchen to double-check the burners were off and the plugs were all off even though she'd done this twice already. She could hear the familiar creak of the heavy doors and already knew it was him that had come in. She hadn't heard pint glasses being placed on the bar or the shuffling of coats and stools. This was someone coming in, not out. Her heart beat heavy in her chest and she hesitated in the doorway of the small kitchen and pretended to busy herself folding tea towels to seem distracted when he would come around the corner to find her.

She heard the gruff acknowledgement from Rab and Stuarty who didn't try for small talk with him anymore and then, "She in here?" as his voice sounded nearer. Teeny turned her back, all of a sudden overcome with shyness that she had been so direct and forward. She pulled another pile of tea towels to start folding.

"Too late for last orders?" he almost whispered, making Teeny genuinely jump even though she knew he'd be coming into the kitchen.

"Hello, hiya. I didn't think you would be in tonight?" She tried for a casual tone. He lifted an incredulous eyebrow and edged in closer leaning against the doorway with his arms folded.

"I couldn't really ignore a text like that, could I? I wanted to look you in the eye and hear you say it to my face," he said with such a serious voice that Teeny could feel her heart pulsate in her throat and her knees soften. She noted his beard had grown in more since she last saw him. It had come in darker around his mouth and chin and she wondered if it would be soft or harsh against her own skin. She remembered, last time, how raw her chin had felt after he left and was relieved no one would be awake when she got home to notice. He wore a grey long-sleeved polo shirt and jeans and it always struck Teeny how smart and out of place he looked in this dive. It had been raining so his silver swept hair had fallen over his forehead and he ran his hand through it to tidy it as he waited for Teeny to respond.

"I don't know what to say, Mark, you've kind of caught me off guard here." She licked her lips and stepped backwards towards the sink. "I like you. More than I should admit to. Fuck, I can't stop thinking about you but then I feel like a total cow because I live with my boyfriend's fucking parents and then you just fuck off and don't come back and leave me wondering what the fuck I'm going to do..." Her hand flew up to her head in exasperation. She had been trying to be discreet and not raise her voice but had squeaked out her last couple of sentences.

"I know. I'm sorry, that was unfair of me to expect you just to let me know immediately," he said softly as he stepped towards her and took her hand away from her head and held it. After a minute or so, he looked intensely into her eyes and practically whispered, "I'm a patient guy, Colette, but I'm not willing to share you. For long..." He added as he closed the gap between them and kissed her.

She held the sink for support and he stroked the inside of her thigh. She tried to keep quiet as his hand roamed under her leggings and into her underwear. She struggled to keep her voice down and let out small gasps of pleasure into his mouth in between kisses. She didn't care that there were three other men a matter of footsteps on the other side of the door.

She didn't care that the harsh, fluorescent light of the kitchen made her look sweaty and unattractive and she didn't care that a man other than her boyfriend had his fingers inside her because it was the most erotic moment of her life to date. She could hear the glasses clink on to the bar.

"Right, wee yin, another for the road when you're ready"... "You still in there, Teeny? Did she go doon the cellar, Rab?" Stuarty called out. Teeny grasped any and every ounce of control she had left in her to respond, "I'm just coming!" before losing control of her senses and tensing against him as the waves rippled over her. She straightened her back and slid out from against the sinks and the two of them simply looked at each other and laughed as she headed back out to sort last orders.

A couple of minutes later, Mark joined her at the bar innocently presenting the pile of tea towels 'Teeny had asked him' to fold for her. She took them and bit her lip trying to conceal her laughter. Auld Tam left ten minutes later with a simple hand in the air and the other fixing his bunnet to signal his departure. The coffin dodgers held off, savouring every last sip of their drinks before shuffling out as well. They were finally alone.

She'd spent the last hour studiously avoiding eye contact so she wouldn't blush but now there were no excuses. She pulled down the shutter and locked it. "You," she finally said. "I want you but I just don't know how to deal with Ryan yet. He'll be fucking gutted, Mark, and I'm just not ready for it. He'll be heartbroken and it'll be all my fault..." she trailed off with guilt weighing heavy on her chest.

"Shh shh." He held her and consoled her. "I'll wait. I'll wait until you figure it out."

She was so intoxicated by him. She breathed in his smell and felt how soft his clothes were and reached up to run her hands through his hair as she kissed him again.

Soft, she thought to herself, his beard was softer this time.

A couple of weeks later, Ryan's parents were headed to the caravan for a long weekend and taking a very reluctant Joanne with them.

This is it, Teeny thought. *I need to tell him now and get it over with.*

She'd texted Mark to let him know and even though he had offered her to stay with him until she sorted herself out, it felt too soon. This seemed a ridiculous notion since they'd spent every day either texting or on the phone. If he picked her up from work, they would either drive around aimlessly just listening to music and talking about everything they loved, everything that scared them and everything in between or they would explore each other's bodies within the confines of his car or in the pub. But she had never set foot in his flat. The notion of this made her feel uneasy. That, in theory, she would be leaving one boyfriend's house for another. She told Mark she would phone her folks but didn't want to follow up on that either. She decided to wing it. Maybe Ryan would be relieved? Maybe he would tell her he too had met someone else and was glad they were no longer living a lie. Maybe he'd let her stay on at his mum's and share a room with Joanne until she got set up with her own place? She shook her head at her ridiculous train of thought.

She had packed a couple of bags of her clothes and looked out all her documents she couldn't afford him burning out of spite like her passport and birth certificate. She put the bags at the back door and sat on the couch waiting for him to come in from work. She heard the van door shut and Ryan call out something undecipherable to his workmate but he was laughing. He walked in and with normal routine, stepped out of his boots shook out of his plastering clothes and adjusted his balls while catching up on any messages on his phone.

"Awright Teen, how's you?" he asked without really looking up. "Fancy phoning suhin' the night, we've got the hoos to ourselves? CHIPS, CHEESE AND DONNER, WE'RE ON IT TIL THE MORA!" he chanted pumping his fist in the air.

Teeny smiled but it only made her feel worse. "Ryan, I-I…" she stammered but Ryan obliviously scooped her up and jumping up and down still chanting. She shoved his arms down. "Ryan, put me down, Ryan! RYAN, fuck sake put me fucking down!"

He complied and made a poor joke about the devil being in her belly this week. She breathed slowly to contain her temper. This was her doing, this was her guilt making her angry, not him.

"I'm leaving," she said softly. "I-I don't want to be with you anymore. I'm really sorry. It's not about you, I just don't think we fit anymore, we kind of just got into this thinking that we should live together and buy a house and get on with it but I don't think that's what I want and I just…" she had started to ramble through her tears.

"Are you having a fucking laugh, Teeny? This isn't funny!" Ryan said quietly but seriously now. She shook her head. "Don't suppose it's anything to do with the auld guy that's been hingin' aboot the Keys?" he asked coolly. Her face flushed a deep red and Ryan didn't need her to answer. "Aye, a thought so. Louis told me I should keep an eye out for some 'silver fox tryin' to cut ma gress' and I laughed thinking not Teeny. Not my Teeny, she'd never do that." He paced the room and vigorously shook his head.

"Have you shagged him?"

Teeny looked to the side, to the door as if looking for someone to rescue her from this conversation. To this question, Ryan needed an answer.

"HAVE YOU FUCKING SHAGGED HIM, TEENY?" he roared.

"Yes," she nodded. "I've slept with him."

He finally sat with his head his hands and was quiet for a long time. "Get ti fuck, Teen. Get out," he said, deflated.

"Ryan, look, I'm sorry," Teeny tried to apologise but a renewed anger had flushed through him and he was back on his feet.

"I said, GET. TO. FUCK!" Storming past her up the stairs into his room. Teeny quickly followed. He was roughly opening drawers and the wardrobe looking for her things to pack for her and send her on her way.

"I've packed already, Ryan," she interrupted. "It's all gone."

He looked at her for a long time as if he was looking at her for the first time.

"You're a fucking coward, Teeny, and an absolute slag. Get the fuck away from me before I lose it!"

She'd seen Ryan shout before but never in temper and never at her. Her shame turned her on her heel and she walked as quickly as she could out the back door with her bags and she tried to ignore the choked sobs of Ryan repeating 'fuck sake' through tears as she gathered her things on the doorstep.

She walked into the Cross Keys and ordered a double Bacardi and cola.

"Fuck sake, how long ye staying?" Darren asked clocking the bags.

"Don't. Please, Darren." He gave her a tight smile and had drawn his own conclusions.

Ryan had punted her out for cheating with that guy, Mark. Everyone knew. She hadn't exactly been discreet. Once she'd nearly finished her drink, Darren had felt brave enough to broach the subject again. "You going back to your folks then?" he asked curiously, knowing what a reprobate Alec was and how miserable Teeny had been living there.

She shrugged. "Dunno yet," she said and sank the rest of her drink.

"What about the new guy?" he asked shyly.

"Fuck. Off. Darren. Alright? Fuck off. Not tonight. I really don't need it. I just want to get drunk and get this day to fuck!" She practically seethed at him.

"Well, *that* I can help with," he responded and set out another drink for her, pushing back her ten-pound note towards her signalling it was on him. Teeny felt bad for chewing him out like that but at the same time, who the fuck did he think he was calling her out so direct? *Nosy cunt,* she thought.

As she moved on to her third drink on an empty stomach, she could feel anxiety swirl in her stomach. Had she made the right call? Was everyone talking about her? Did they all hate her now? How had she ended up here, this person? She ran to the toilet to be violently sick, the orangey brown foam filling the bowl and pouring from Teeny like an exorcism. As she spat out the final remnants of spewy phlegm, she rested her head against the cubicle and started to cry.

What have I done? she questioned her judgements and her thought processes over the last few weeks. She thought of Mark and how he was the only kind face she could rely on right now. He wouldn't scold her. He would take her away from the judgemental eyes and harsh whispery tones she convinced herself she could hear. She pulled her phone out.

"I've done it. I've ended it. Please come get me. I'm in the pub." Seconds later, he'd replied telling her he was on his way and to come outside to get him. She rinsed her mouth out with water and splashed her face and neck. She would need to change her top for some of the splashes had landed on her t-shirt. As she returned to her homeless cart of possessions at the bar, she set about putting her rucksack on and pulling the bags onto her arms.

"See you for your shift on Sunday then, pal?" Darren offered as a kind of peace offering, she supposed.

"Yep. See you, Sunday." She nodded nervously.

"Take care, wee yin, eh?" he said quieter and leaning closer to her.

"I will," she responded with a kinder tone, "now fuck off back to serving, ya lazy bastard." She smiled and laughed and he gave her the middle finger and walked away. Balance restored again in their odd friendship.

Mark arrived in under ten minutes as if he'd been waiting on her contact, knowing she'd need his rescue at some point. He helped her put the bags in the car and she helped herself to three or four polos from his glove compartment as she climbed in the passenger seat, suddenly quite self-conscious that she should be putting on some airs and graces to impress the new man in her life. Mark pulled away and smiled while stroking her knee, telling Teeny how beautiful she was.

"Beautiful, you must be joking, I'm a hot mess and I'm boufin eh sick and I'm the biggest slag in this fucking village…why are you still smiling?" she asked, slightly annoyed with him.

"'Cause you're my hot mess. All mine. I'm going to look after you, sweetheart, and you're no slag. You were just with the wrong person, that's all."

She didn't really believe that part but it was nice to hear and she needed it badly in that moment.

"Please just come stay with me for a bit. I don't want to you living in some temporary homeless shithole, Colette. You can stay with me and do whatever you want to do to sort yourself out. No pressure. Honestly."

She conceded with a smile and a nod, afraid to speak for fear of crying again.

"Brilliant," he said, looking relieved, "let's go home then."

8. 5 November 2018

They'd sat in awkward silence with Alec while Denise poured tea and Alec slurped at his Tennent's. It's not how Teeny would have done it. This first meeting should have happened on neutral territory. The pub maybe. She felt exposed in their tiny kitchen with her drunk father and her socially inept mother. Embarrassed even. Mark knew what Alec was like, he'd seen it first hand and Teeny had already talked about her mother's poor mental health. Her quiet nature.

One night, early on in their relationship, they had lay in the dark together talking about their families and their very different childhoods. Both only children with no siblings. His father had died when he was a teenager and he didn't seem to speak of him fondly. His mother was now in a nursing home and he spoke of her much more softly. Her dementia meant she would sometimes forget she was a resident and try to help administer medicines and take over during the bingo nights. Some habits so deeply engrained from a lifetime career of nursing herself. Teeny laughed involuntarily at the thought of her trying to take over and apologised for her insensitivity, then he laughed too.

Teeny told him about her parents' poorly disguised dislike for each other. How, when she was ten, her mum was pregnant but lost the baby and after that spent days at a time in bed and hardly ever went out anymore and just always seemed so sad. Her throat caught as she said the last words and Mark wiped the tear away from her cheek and kissed her on her bare shoulder. They lay quietly after that, the time of reflection making them both feel raw and defensive about the people who had raised and shaped them.

Teeny played with the pattern on the tea plate awkwardly as Denise asked Mark about his work. He had been so charming and talkative and Teeny was grateful for it. It took the light over to him and away from her and her family's inability to carry out basic small talk. It also meant more time passed where Teeny didn't need to have the conversation out loud that she'd been practicing in her head. That would need to wait until they went home. Home. Mark had brought his car and parked it outside the Cross Keys to wait for Alec's inevitable arrival after work.

Teeny excused herself from the table to gather her belongings from her makeshift bedroom and included some clothes she'd left behind and the copy of the *The Catcher in the Rye*. She wanted to take the time to read it properly, having devoured it so quickly to distract herself this last day. They walked out the door together shouting goodbye down the hall to her parents rather than traditional wave off at the door including sweet goodbye kisses and shaken hands.

Teeny took in large breaths and let the cold air cleanse her chest, she felt as though she had been taking shallow breaths ever since she could hear her father's voice as he came home with Mark in tow. She held tightly onto the rucksack with both hands, avoiding the possibility of her hand skimming his as they took the short walk to his car. She couldn't trust herself.

Rage now sparked and flinted in her gut as she practiced her speech in her head. She stole glances at him as they walked in silence and his face was relaxed and he wasn't giving anything away. Was he relieved she was OK or was he faking it until they got home where he would lose it with her for leaving? Had she completely fooled herself and betrayed herself by throwing herself onto the spider's web?

He took her bag from her to put in the boot as she climbed in the passenger seat. The seats were cold and the seatbelt buckle colder still. She could see her breath inside the car and eagerly awaited the engine coming on so she could warm her hands and legs. Teeny thought about the first time she'd been in his car back in May time. He'd insisted on driving her home the short distance to Ryan's parents since there had been a lot of fighting after an Auld Firm match during the day. The pub was packed and a couple of unusual faces in poorly concealed Celtic tops and a defeat for Rangers was a guaranteed recipe for madness. Mark hadn't even been in that night but Teeny had text him to give him the gossip of the daft Celtic fan with the kicked-in teeth and the idiots that had been put out for the act of violence swearing they would be back to 'tan the windaes' later on. Teeny had heard it all before and knew eight times out of ten it was an empty threat. Mark was outside waiting as Teeny and Darren came out from under the shutter and pulled it down to lock it. She'd clocked his headlights and lied to Darren to walk on since Ryan was coming to meet her. Darren plugged his earphones in and nodded, marching off in the opposite direction, oblivious.

Butterflies in her heart and stomach told her she was happy to see him. She tried to act nonchalant anyway.

"Thought I told you I'd be fine?" she scolded with a raised eyebrow.

He looked sheepish. "I just wanted to make sure, that's all. And I could be pretty confident I'd be the only one here to do it."

Her instincts wanted to defend Ryan, to chide Mark for being unfair to him but she didn't want to, she was relieved he was there. She sat in the passenger seat and soaked in the smell of the car. His aftershave, the sea breeze pine tree hanging. The polo mint he had in his mouth. She gave him some rough instructions to the address and he started the engine. It was a warm, close night and the roads were empty. Mark continued on the main road and had missed the left turn. Excitement coursed through her stomach and thighs as he continued to drive under the skew brig towards the business park.

"Are you lost?" She giggled.

A smile crept over his face and he continued to drive towards the secluded car park.

Today, though, the drive back to Mark's flat was painfully quiet. They went inside and Teeny dumped the rucksack in the hall and pulled her phone out to go find her charger.

"I thought you were dead," Mark said almost inaudibly from the lounge door.

She wasn't ready to talk, her head was swimming and she hadn't been able to gauge his mood all day and now he was blocking her only exit from the room. She walked over to the floor lamp and switched it on and some of the cabinet under lighters in the kitchen to break up the darkness. She wanted to buy time to think of how to start her response but Mark continued before she had to.

"I woke up and you were just…fucking…gone." He started to cry softly.

It automatically tugged at Teeny's need to go to him to mould herself to him to make him whole again. But she stood still and waited for his rage.

"I thought I'd hurt you so bad you'd went in an ambulance or something but then I saw the note on the fridge and saw your charger still on the counter."

Teeny noted the board had been completely cleared now. She slowly nodded.

"When I didn't hear from the police, I assumed you had gone to your folks."

The police? she thought. It hadn't even occurred to her to contact the police to get him in trouble. She didn't want to hurt him like that. She tried to keep a blank expression to keep focussed.

"I'm so ashamed I hurt you like that." He sniffed. "I haven't been able to eat or sleep with the guilt of it all."

Teeny already knew that was a lie. She had stood over him in the dark watching him sleep dreamlessly before she left.

"I'm going to get help, for my temper. I never want to hurt you again and would do anything not to lose you. If that's what you want me to do, I'll do it."

She continued to stand quietly. No longer by choice but with anger. She had wanted him to get help. She'd had the request prepared in her speech, for his anger, his jealousy, his violence. But now, she felt cheated. He'd stolen her power chip. She was going to tell him to get help or she would leave for good but he'd already thought of it and fixed it himself. She was angry that he had stolen it from her and angry that she had never got to shout and scream for being hurt in the first place. She'd taken less violence in the pub and thrown punches back and screamed in the faces of men twice the size of her. It had felt good. But this time, she had cried and she had run away and she had missed him after she ran. *How fucked up is that?* she questioned herself.

"I love you, Mark," she started.

"I love you too, Col—" he started.

"I wasn't finished," Teeny interrupted his response and his face quickly flitted between relief to anger to confusion in under two seconds. "I love you, Mark, but if you lay a hand on me again, I swear I will leave then call the police and I won't come back. And yes. You will get help. For you though. Not for me. OK? OK." She answered herself and stormed past him to the master bedroom full of confidence she'd plucked out of thin air. Then terror set in. He could come in to attack her at any moment and it was a fight she simply was not ready for. She'd been bluffing and hoped he didn't know it. He followed her to the bedroom and nodded, silently agreeing to her 'demands'.

Once she had assured herself she would be safe, she started to shuffle out of the hoodie and jeans she had over worn. She felt gross and had been sweating profusely since she came inside. She stood in her underwear enjoying Mark's eyes on her, making sure the bedside lamp was on so he could see his artwork on her legs. She took her time bringing out a towel and her t-shirt and shorts for bed. She slowly peeled off her underwear kicking it up into her hands and dropped it in the washing basket in the en suite. Lifting her towel from the bed, she excused herself, passed Mark who stood, still in his jacket, dazed in the bedroom doorway.

She let the shower run for a minute or so before stepping in to its delicious warmth. She lathered her hair up and took extra care to condition it slowly and comb it through with her fingers. She shaved under her arms and noted she still had a good couple of weeks before needing to book a wax appointment with Pauline. She used the coconut scented shower crème in her hands so she could clean her legs and body more gently without hurting the bruises. She turned the water off and patted herself dry with the fluffy towel and roughly towel dried her hair. Walking back through into the bedroom, she dropped the towel on the floor and set about moisturising her body and combing all her hair through. Mark now perched at the end of the bed had taken his coat off but looked as if he was awaiting his appointment with the head teacher. He kept his eyes down.

Teeny was enjoying herself too much now. He'd never been so quiet before. It turned her on as if she might have actually shifted some of the power into her own corner. She pulled on the t-shirt and shorts and lay on her side of the bed staring at the pattern in the wallpaper. Mark pulled his weight onto his side and studied the bruises on Teeny's legs. He gingerly put his hand towards her to seek her permission to touch her then traced rings around each of their full scale. He kissed them each softly and slowly lingering over her knees which he knew she loved. Teeny let out an involuntary sigh and she flexed her toes. He kissed her legs more sensually then and planted kisses over her hips, where there were no bruises. He moved up towards her stomach which was still quite tender, kissing her and nudging the t-shirt out of his way with this nose. He moaned her name as he kissed her stomach. If this was happening, she had to take her head away from the other night, the pain from his chin and forearms leaning on her tender legs and stomach were only a reminder of where she did not want to be mentally right now. She gently pushed him onto his back, sliding her t-shirt off as she did, then straddled him. She rested her chin on her own forearms which were crossed over his chest and she sighed again. "I'm sorry. I was a horrible dick and I'll never do it again," he said while sliding the wet strands of hair back from her face.

"I know, it's OK," she conceded but wasn't sure if she fully believed herself and couldn't look him in the eye while saying it so shuffled further away from his face to help him get undressed. She enjoyed his stunned helpless look as she took him in her mouth unexpectedly. He pulled her hair 'round to the side to better see her face so she moved onto her side to hide her face again.

"Come here," he almost pleaded and she could feel the pinching of his summons under her jaw and on her shoulders. She complied and he pulled her up to his face as they kissed deeply. He roughly pulled her shorts down from one leg and he held her face close to his, no matter how subtly she tried to shake away and thrusted from beneath her until he came.

He relaxed his grip and whispered into her hair, "What did I do to deserve you, eh?" before helping her ease off him then went to the bathroom. She no longer felt as powerful and as confident. She felt a little embarrassed for herself and stupid but mostly frustrated.

"Will I order some food?" he shouted through from the lounge.

"Yep, sounds good. Whatever you fancy," she answered as she continued to stare at the wallpaper.

"You need to eat something," Mark interrupted her distracted thoughts. She sat at the breakfast bar pushing the noodles around her plate, watching bright, colourful fireworks intermittently light up the sky outside.

"I think I've had enough," she said but continued to eat a few more mouthfuls so he would stop staring at her. He looked away when she began to chew. He excused himself to go and iron his shirt for work in the morning and she set about clearing up the plates.

She thought about her mother and how tired she looked today. Denise was only 44, two years younger than Mark but looked at least a decade older than him. Her brown hair once sat so perfectly straight and glossy on her shoulders now so sat limp and grey. Reflective of how she spoke and carried herself in general. She wished she could fix her. Wished they could sit and drink and giggle together and talk about boys and college and they could go on shopping trips like normal mothers and daughters. Nothing about their relationship was like normal mother and daughters. She cringed remembering the school nurse mimicking how to use a sanitary towel when she started her first period. She remembered thinking she was pregnant and losing a baby like Denise had and didn't want to upset her mother by mentioning that she was bleeding. Still being a virgin at the time, this was impossible, the patronising look on that smug bint nurse's face told her that. Despite everything, she had somehow ended up closer to her father since she physically saw him at least four times a week, by default. They rarely spoke other than his signalling that his jar was empty or to tell her another distant relative or villager had died.

"I think it's clean now." Mark's voice snapped her out of her thoughts.

"What?" she asked, startled and confused.

"The plate, I think it's clean – you've had it in your hand about ten minutes," he explained.

Teeny rinsed it off noting that the water in the sink had cooled off and Mark had returned from the bedroom and was at the breakfast bar sitting on his phone.

When did he come back in? she wondered to herself. She dried her hands and took her phone off of charge.

"Thought we could watch this thing on BBC4 about Otis Redding, you like him, eh?" he asked as he made his way over to the sofa.

"Mmm hmm." She smiled but really, she was exhausted and wanted to go to bed. She wanted to cling to this feeling more though. This normality; eating dinner, cleaning dishes, watching TV. The atmosphere in the flat felt calm, cosy. Mark had lit a couple of the candles 'round the fireplace and turned the TV on.

She quickly texted her mum: *"Thanks for letting me stay last night. It was good to see you, I've missed you. Love you xx"* and set her phone down on the coffee table. She sat down next to Mark and tucked her feet up, pulling the throw over her legs and nestling onto his chest while the soulful music and lyrics and talking heads blurred past on the screen before her. She had almost nodded off when her phone vibrated. She knew it would be her mother but she still panicked knowing she had no control over what she would write back or if she would comment anything about Mark. And she knew he would lift her phone first. He easily unlocked the phone and having glanced at the text first to proofread, showed her the screen *"U 2 doll"*. She nodded in recognition that she'd read the message and he could return her phone to the table. She cradled her head back into the crook of his shoulder and chest, not to fall back asleep but to hide her watering eyes.

A wave of sadness flowed over her and her mouth and chest hurt to try and stop herself from sobbing. Did she mean so little to her family or was this more about her mother's stunted emotional availability? Her mother never phoned her, rarely text her back and barely spoke to her when they were around each other. Mark on the other hand had come searching for her after barely 48 hours after being away from her. He had his faults but he was going to get help and at least he loved her enough to care about where she was and how she was. She nodded off again and awoke to the smell of the freshly blown out candles and Mark rubbing her arm to tell her to come to bed.

She regretted the nap on the couch because now she lay wide awake. She watched as the odd passing car in the distance created looming shadows that climbed the wall then disappeared again. It was after 2 am now and she still couldn't sleep. Teeny promised herself she would contact student services tomorrow to sort out her coursework, to get a better handle on how badly she was fucking up. She thought about what she would say, what excuses she could use and how much she really didn't want to go. She was afraid to be told it was too late, she had missed too much and failed too much by default. The humiliation. She sighed again and shifted her weight onto her side to slide closer to Mark. She put her nose against his back and breathed in his scent and tuned in to his breathing. She tried to match his breathing to calm her own. After a few minutes, she shifted again to the other side, trying to help her mind run away from the course of thoughts that seemed to be speeding up in a loop and she could feel anxiety flurry in her chest and sweat secrete on her palms and face.

"Fuck sake, Colette, will you lie still?" Mark's snarl came out of the darkness.

She stretched her palm out to the bedside table to feel its cool, hard surface but didn't breathe a word. It was 4 am before she could feel the weight of her eyelids take over from the panic that had gripped the steering wheel of her mind all night.

9. 26 November 2018

Numb. She rubbed again. Still numb. Teeny tried to physically grip to her reality by running her hands by her sides and concentrating on the material beneath them; soft carpet, hard stone, wood. A nervous habit she had picked up when her mind raced. She couldn't feel the bedsheets beneath her hands now and frantically rubbed them to try to calm the panic in her throat. Like boiling blood making its way up like vomit, it scorched into her face and hair and she could feel the heat in her neck, ears and scalp. She heaved in the air and couldn't focus. Her chest was so tight and her failsafe calming technique wasn't working. She couldn't feel the sheet; she was going to die. She slumped off the bed and lay in the foetal position running her toes along the carpet like the hand of a grandfather clock. *Tick tock. Tock Tick. Tick tick tock.*

Slowly, she could feel her breath slow and her chest relax. She felt incredibly sick and her stomach cramped so she knew she would need to get up and run to the toilet. She rested her head against the cool sink as she sat there and her stomach completed its rinse cycle. She reached for the hand towel and soaked it in cold water wrapping it around her neck as if she had just fought 12 rounds. She sipped some cold water from the tap and lay down on the cold tiles and tried to empty her mind and pull back the derailed train that was her thoughts.

It was supposed to be a simple appointment. Routine even. Her contraceptive pill had run out and she needed more. The smarmy receptionist told her she'd need to be seen by the doctor since it had been six months since her last review. She'd had to wait nearly two weeks for the appointment which meant she'd had an unplanned period. The first one she'd had in six months and she felt quite literally drained. The cramps had been worse than she'd ever remembered and she just couldn't seem to stop crying. She was aware that she was coming across as whiny and needy to Mark and it was wearing thin. He'd kept to his promise and hadn't lifted his hands to her but he was irritable and sarcastic and Teeny felt like she couldn't do right for doing wrong.

At work, she willed the hours away so she could scuttle back to the safety and shelter of the flat where she wouldn't need to make conversation or use her best customer service smile. She was exhausted. She sat in the waiting room waiting for her name to be called and reread the email from college on her phone. She mentally highlighted the phrases 'sorry to advise that' and 'hopefully you can return in the future'. She'd royally fucked it. Nothing more than a barmaid. There was something freeing about this, Teeny felt. At least she didn't need to worry about not going in anymore, she didn't have to make excuses to Mark why she had to be there in the library to study later to try and pick her marks up. She didn't have to explain to her friends why she was bruised and skittish about getting home so early. There was some peace in it for her.

"Colette Holmes… Colette Holmes?" The male doctor stood in front of the waiting room waiting for Teeny to catch on he meant her and she should follow.

"Hi, I'm one of the locum doctors, Dr Donaldson. What can I do for you?"

She noted from his diary on his desk his full name was Lesley Donaldson. She'd never met a man called Lesley before. She'd explained she needed a review for her pill and he dutifully took her weight and blood pressure and asked the usual questions; "Do you suffer from regular headaches?"

"…yes."

"Do you get any pain in your legs?"

Teeny subconsciously stroked her almost healed bruise on her thigh. "No."

"And do you feel well in yourself?"

Teeny nodded but the tears had already started to spill over her cheeks. "I'm OK, I just…I just feel so all over the place right now. I'm struggling to keep my thoughts in check."

The doctor nodded encouragingly so she continued, "I feel like I might be losing it. Like I can't concentrate and don't want to do anything anymore and feel like I'm afraid of my own shadow." The familiar feeling of despair pulled her heart down with gravity and she shook her head as if trying to shake away the fear and hopelessness that were held over her like a plastic bag over her face. "I'm really sorry," she apologised, wiping her face. "I think it's just 'cause I've been on the pill so long and then I've had a break so the hormones will be everywhere, that'll be it, eh?"

She looked to the doctor for confirmation that that was all that was she needed. Just her pill. Then she'd be fine.

Dr Donaldson went on to ask Teeny how her sleeping pattern was, how often she drank, how often she ate and had she ever thought about harming herself or taking her own life. She hadn't but she had certainly thought it would all be a lot easier if she just wasn't here. The thought was frightening in itself. Dr Donaldson had recommended Teeny stay on in the waiting room to get some bloods taken by the nurse just to double check her thyroid and some other things as these levels can impact one's mood. He also spoke to her about possibly starting some anti-depressants. Teeny thought of her mother.

No. No way. I'm not depressed. I'm not that bad, not like her. I'm fine it's just been a mad year. I'm fine, she thought to herself as she turned down the tablets.

He gave her a couple of contact cards for websites for self-help material and told her the nurse would be with her in 15 minutes before handing her the prescription for the pill.

She put her earphones back in and played some music, letting the lyrics waltz over her shoulders massaging away the tension and she'd just started to breathe easier after her appointment when the overwhelming floral scent of Viktor and Rolf hit her, almost choking her. She looked to see who would be wearing such a strong perfume in the fucking doctors. Chloe Thompson. If there was ever a real-life imitation of Miss Piggy from the Muppets, this was her.

Teeny had disliked her since High School but even more so later on when she would bump into her when she was still with Ryan. Chloe had always held a torch for him and would pout her big moon face at him whenever they were in Morries. She would praise his efforts on the pool table and reapply lipstick after every drink making sure she always looked picture perfect. Teeny would teasingly call him 'Kermy' in her best Miss Piggy voice when they would go home and Ryan would admonish her for her unnecessary cruelty.

"She's harmless, Teen," he would tell her.

She knew it but she could still slag her off for being a fud.

"Oh my god, hiya Teeny, how's you?"

Teeny caught as she sighed, taking her earphones out. "Awright Chloe, how's you?"

Chloe had looked a little awkward and a little heavier than usual and after a proper look, Teeny had realised she was having a piglet.

"16 weeks," Chloe beamed, answering the question in Teeny's head.

"Oh magic, congratulations, Chloe, how you keeping?" she'd asked but Chloe answered a question in her own head as if she would explode if she didn't say it.

"It's Ryan's, by the way. The baby. Ryan's the dad. I thought you should hear it from me. You know what this place is like for gossip," she finished with a tight awkward smile.

Teeny smiled and thought her heart might burst.

"Chloe Thompson… Chloe Thompson?" Saved by the midwife summoning Chloe for her appointment.

"Take care Chloe, you and the wee one…and the big yin." She smiled as Chloe waved goodbye and shifted out of her oversized pink bubble jacket.

She didn't feel jealous or hurt. It was actually pretty perfect. She could see Ryan building the cot and buying the tiniest size of the Falkirk strip available. She could see him being the daft daddy and Chloe would adore him forever. It somehow lifted some of the guilt she'd been torturing herself with. After her own name was called, she sat for the bloods to be taken then hurried back into town to get home and safe as quick as possible as she could feel the assault of her own mind coming, the blind panic and all that went with it.

She lay on the bathroom floor recovering from her panic attack for the best part of an hour before finally pulling herself up. It was darker now outside and it was a miserable evening. Mark would be back from work soon. She decided to try to cook some dinner to distract herself. She stirred the pasta as she heard Mark's keys turn in the door. He looked surprised to see her cooking and appear brighter than she had been in the last few weeks. He snaked his arms around her waist and peered over her shoulder into the pots.

"Did you get on OK at the doc's then?" he asked.

"Yep, all sorted. They took some bloods too just to check my thyroid and stuff in case that's what's affecting my mood."

Mark looked slightly surprised and questioned, "Did *she ask* about how you've been feeling like?"

Teeny decided not to correct the doctor's gender. "Yes, it's part of the review along with other general health questions," she said in a conversational tone, sensing his mood grow tense.

"Nosy wankers they doctors, honestly," he retorted.

"You go in for some pills to stop you getting pregnant and they want your fucking life story? What did you tell them? That you're fucking miserable all the time, that I'm the bad bastard who makes you miserable?"

"No," she responded sadly. "I just said I wasn't feeling great but it'll just be the change in hormones. I never mentioned you," she defended.

Mark who had been pacing around as he took his coat off finally sat on one of the stools and watched Teeny stirring the sauce.

"Nosy wankers," he repeated. "They always want to overcomplicate everything and overthink everything."

Teeny thought he was maybe referring to his own recent experience with his new counsellor for his anger issues rather than her own GP.

"Is your next appointment tomorrow? With the counsellor?" she asked tentatively.

His face hardened. "I cancelled it. It's a lot of nonsense. I know I've got a temper but it was one time I've lost control like that. Once. I've never hurt you like that before and I said I won't again. I don't need some wee tit in a tweed waistcoat asking me about my childhood and my relationship with my parents to know that punching your girlfriend is bad."

Mark continued to stare at her to wait for a response. Teeny turned around to grab the colander from the cupboard to drain the pasta. His tone was so final. This wasn't up for discussion. He had never acknowledged it so verbally before, 'punching your girlfriend'. Teeny wondered if he meant that was the worst part but the other stuff was OK, the questioning, the shouting, the slapping and shoving? As long as it wasn't a punch?

"So? Does this mean you're leaving me or will you stay and we can sort this together?" He returned behind her sweeping her hair around one shoulder so he could kiss the other while holding her. The last three weeks had been pretty hellish but that was more about how she was feeling rather than his treatment of her. He hadn't hit her since she left to stay at her parents so maybe once she sorted herself out and gave herself a bit of a shake, things would be better?

She didn't want to lose him. She wanted things to go back how they were, in the beginning. He'd been so kind, gentle and attentive. They would talk for hours and slow dance in the lounge which she found a bit cringey at first but as she relaxed into it, she loved it. He'd made her feel more alive and 'seen' and loved than she probably ever had. He made her feel important and desirable and grown up. He'd never called her wee yin or kiddo or even Teeny, apart from the first night they met. She loved him and the thought of being apart from him, especially now, the way she was feeling most days, terrified her more than his anger ever had. She lifted one of his hands from his clasp and kissed it.

"We'll sort it together." She smiled and stepped away to get plates to serve their meal.

After they ate, they both sat in silence wondering how to restart the conversation. Teeny rhythmically tapped her bare foot against the breakfast bar as her feet slightly swung from the barstool, not quite tall enough to reach the floor. She swept the baguette crumbs into her hands and lifted tiny pieces of food that weren't there while nervously glancing at Mark.

"What is it?" he said finally.

"What *did* you talk about with the counsellor? Did you tell him you had—" she stammered, hesitating about being so direct, "had hit me?"

He sat back on the stool rubbing his legs and breathing out through his nose visibly trying to control his tone. He paused for long time to carefully consider his answer, whether he wanted to be honest or not.

"I said I was sorry, Colette. I really don't see the point in bringing it up again. Are you trying to hurt me with this, is that what you want?"

Teeny regretted bringing it up but knew she might not get the opportunity again. "I know you're sorry and I'm not trying to hurt you or make this worse. I just wanted to know why it was so bad that you wouldn't want to stick it out to get help?" she said with her palms out, face up in a subordinate fashion.

"I know that I'm fine, that's why. I don't need 'help help' I'm not a fucking psycho Colette, Jesus!" Watching Teeny's eyes tear up, he lowered his voice again. "He asked about my folks, my childhood, that sort of shite. I'm just not into it. My dad was a proper bad bastard, I don't like talking about it."

He shook his head at the ugly memories and the displeasure of describing them now. Teeny wanted to console him and his inner child but sat and continued to listen, the irony of his description of the abuse not lost on her.

"Anyway, I'm nothing like him, far from it. Fuck, I don't accuse you of being like your mum every time you shed a tear, do I?" he blurted out, his eyes getting wider and his voice louder.

Teeny took the words like a knife in her ribs. "That's not fair, Mark. They are not the same thing," she spat out in frustration, feeling her tears betray her and fall hot and heavy down her face like he had summoned them himself to prove his point.

"Aren't they?" he continued cruelly.

"No, they're fucking not!" she started to shout feeling herself become defensive, remembering the offer of anti-depressants earlier that day. "I didn't say you were like your dad; I know fuck all about him. I just think you need to

110

acknowledge your shitty behaviour goes a bit beyond one punch in the stomach and maybe you need to talk to someone about how to *not* do that."

She'd climbed off her stool feeling her own temper rising but preparing herself for potential violence.

"Oh, is that right? Quite the psychologist, are we?" he said mockingly. "Maybe you should study that instead next year, if they let you back in." He let his cruel taunt fall in the silence between them.

"You're a tosser," Teeny responded with her voice shaking with hurt.

He pulled a mock sympathy expression, "And you're a barmaid, sweetheart."

Teeny turned and stomped out of the room, confused about how this conversation had ended up about her own failings but she knew her words were failing her and her emotions betraying her. She walked into the bedroom, hesitating in the hall whether she should just keep heading out the door. She slammed the bedroom door closed and slid down the back of it to sit, in case he came to reprimand her for her childish behaviour. He didn't, she could hear him turn on the TV and pour himself another glass of wine.

As she rose off of the floor, she took a look at herself in the mirrored wardrobe, her face blotchy and pink, her hair scooped up in a lank ponytail. Maybe she was turning into her mum. She pulled her phone from her pocket and checked her last message to Ashley which was at least a month ago.

"Fancy that catch up drink?" she texted. She quickly flicked through the wardrobe and checked the weather outside, the response from Ashley came.

"Fuck yeh – Rialtos? 8?"

111

She confirmed she'd be there and Teeny felt the spark of excitement in her gut. She missed her friend and she missed dressing up. She picked some skinny black jeans and ankle boots and opted for her purple fitted jumper since it was baltic outside. She used some dry shampoo and back combed her hair to give it some life and tried to style a makeshift quirky bun. She took extra care to use the liquid eyeliner, it had been a while so she was a bit rusty and she put some lipstick on. She felt a buzz already but then realised she would need to go back into the lounge to tell Mark she was off out and to collect her handbag from the breakfast bar. She exhaled slowly with her hand on the doorknob before quickly walking into the lounge and lifting her bag before telling Mark she was 'away out to get Ashley' to the back of his head.

"The fuck are you talking about?" he asked leaning over the couch, glass in hand.

"I'm away to meet Ashley for a drink. Is that a problem?"

He squinted his eyes at her defiant stance. "Will Michael be there?" he asked.

She told him "No" but she couldn't be sure that Ashley wouldn't invite him along without her knowledge.

"Then fine, see you later."

She nodded her goodbye, still upset with him for his cruel taunts and left before he asked any further questions or gave her any grief. She got to the pub first and ordered herself a Bacardi and Ashley a gin for her arrival. She checked her phone and sure enough, Mark had texted.

"Have a good night, sorry I was a tosser. Don't be late though, I have work in the morning x."

She didn't respond and Ashley came bouncing in the bar squealing with delight at the sight of her friend, finally out for a drink. Four drinks later, the women had covered Teeny's departure from college and how gutted Ashley was she wouldn't be there anymore. Teeny had mentioned Ryan's pending fatherhood.

"That's fucking mental, man. Mental. Good on him though I guess, that…he's happy?" she looked to Teeny to check that was OK to say.

"Yeh, of course, good on him, I'm glad he's happy too. He deserves it," she added a little sadder than she meant to sound out loud.

"And what about you and Mark, how are things?" Ashley had asked.

Teeny knew it was coming, the 'girl talk'. They hadn't seen each other out with college since they had bumped into each other on her birthday.

"Yeh, good. Things are good." She nodded enthusiastically.

"He seems quite *intense,*" Ashley attempted for humorous curiosity and raised her eyebrow.

Teeny offered a small giggle to let her friend know no offense had been taken.

"He's just more serious, I guess," she responded.

"More mature and all that?" Ashley pressed, letting a smile creep over her lips. "Never really took you for the sugar daddy type, Teen." She then allowed herself to laugh; they both did.

"Oh, fuck off, it's not like that, I'm not like that, I really love him," Teeny chided her friend jokingly.

"And the sex?" Ashley continued; she was making sure she got it all out there for fear she wouldn't get Teeny on her own again for a while.

Teeny and Ashley had always had open and honest conversations about their sex lives, Ashley having more experience in quantity and Teeny picking up all her tips and tricks and hilarious one-night stand stories along the way. This somehow felt wrong to share though, Teeny blushed and looked down towards her drink. Ashley teasing, "You've got a proper fucking beamer, it must be good!"

"Let's just say it's as 'intense' as he is," Teeny answered and they both laughed and Ashley started to share the story of her latest Tinder disaster.

In the bathroom, Teeny looked at herself in the mirror. She noted that her cheeks were slightly rosy from the alcohol but she also felt a fuzzy glow from giggling and laughing. It felt really nice. She remembered to text Mark and pulled out her phone to a couple of messages from him both along the lines 'is it just you two that are out'. She decided just to phone him. The pub had been quiet and she would just say she was having a good time and she would be home soon.

"Why didn't you text back?" was his greeting as he picked up.

"Because I'm out with my friend enjoying myself and didn't want to be stuck to my phone, it's rude," she answered, built up with confidence from the Bacardi.

"Charming. When will you be home then?" he followed up with.

She was walking out back into the bar to finish up the call when Michael who had appeared and was ordering drinks with Ashley and felt the need to greet her by shouting her name as if she was at the opposite side of fucking George Square to him.

"Are you fucking kidding me, Colette? You said it was just you two?" Mark snarled down the phone.

Fright and embarrassment seized her stomach. "It-it was, he's just shown up while I've been in the toilet. I didn't know he was coming. Ashley probably texted him," she stuttered.

In that moment, she hated Ashley. Hated her for inviting him then hated Michael for showing up and for shouting her name and for Ashley again for agreeing to come out and then finally herself for even coming out. For naively thinking she could just have a spontaneous drink without this exhausting carousel to endure.

"Colette, I am really fucking trying here but you need to do your part. If this is to work, I need to trust you too. Trust that you'll not run out the door into the arms of some other dick the minute I say something you don't like. Come home. Now!" he said with finality.

Teeny wondered what she must have looked like; wide-eyed, clutching her phone, hovering around the toilets to her friends who were holding her drink for her waiting on her coming back.

"I can't just leave, Mark. I-I don't know how to explain that to them." She could feel her eyes beginning to water with her anxiety returning.

"Grow up, Colette, tell them you've had enough and you're coming home." His words were starting to seethe and she could tell even through the phone he'd be talking through his teeth as he spoke.

She thought about their conversation earlier, about his promise not to hurt her. He'd need to learn to trust her and she'd need to trust that he wasn't going to hit her whenever he got angry.

"No, Mark, I've not had enough. I'm having a drink with my friends who I've not seen for ages and probably won't for a long time since I got fucked out of college. I'll be home soon. I love you." She quickly hung up so she didn't need to hear his response and try to control her shaking before she walked back to the bar.

After a couple of drinks, Michael and Ashley had started talking about course material for which Teeny had little to no reference. The embarrassment of failing started to creep into her brain and she could feel herself become dizzy and too warm.

"I'm just going to step outside…for fresh air," she half shouted since the bar had filled up and there was music on.

She half-waved, half-saluted in her drunken state and wandered out to sit in the bus shelter outside. She roughly rubbed her face to try to sober up and centre herself somewhat. The fresh air had escalated her inebriation and all the stars in the sky started to vibrate and dance about a bit. Her muscles in her face felt numb and she could feel herself swaying about.

A voice beside her asked if she had a lighter.

"No," she had answered.

"You want some company then, doll?" his second question.

"Nope," she responded as politely as she could.

"You'll end up freezing out here with no jaiket on," he answered and simultaneously put his arm around Teeny's shoulder.

The weight of his arm around her made her feel tiny, like she couldn't hold him up and would slide off the slim bus shelter bench to the floor. She clumsily tried to shake him off but he just readjusted his arm and began slavering pish in her ear about the constellations in the sky.

"Colette. Move. Get in the car," said a voice from the road that she recognised instantly. She didn't hesitate or even think to go back in for her coat or say goodbye to her friends. She simply stood up and climbed into the passenger seat like a child would after being found running away from home.

10. 27 November 2018

She had cooled down now and felt all the crisp winter air on her. She couldn't warm herself up and Mark's commanding of her to get into the car had sobered her up pretty quickly. She regretted leaving her coat and felt guilty knowing her friends would be worried about her. Having seen the two missed calls from Ashley and one from a number she didn't have saved, she assumed Michael had also tried to call to make sure their friend was OK.

"Sorry, took a whitey and walked 'round to the taxi rank... lightweight xx" was the best and probably most plausible text she could come up with and at least she had checked in that she was alright.

Teeny turned her phone off for fear of any comebacks either of them may have, aware that Mark, who hadn't said a word was glancing at her lit-up phone from the driver's seat as he made his way through the quiet streets. His flat was only a short drive from the main anchor of the town centre but he seemed to be taking the scenic route home, tightening and loosening his grip on the wheel.

"Where are we going, it's late. Shouldn't we get home?" Teeny asked, feeling panicked as they seemed to drive in the opposite direction of the flat.

He didn't answer. He eventually pulled into the industrial site alongside the canal which was deserted and poorly lit. As he slowed down the car, Teeny could feel fear curdling in her gut and the blood drain away from her face and hands. She had no idea why he would come here and felt she was perhaps deserving of punishment since she had been drinking with a man he didn't like and didn't know was out with her and then a total stranger was literally hanging off of her when he pulled up alongside them. As he parked the car and let go of the wheel, he took a few deep breaths to himself. Teeny wondered how long it would take for her to outrun him to the main road. Would she make it? Did she want to? Could she fight back this time? The leftover alcohol in her system made her brave and as he reached out to touch her face or cup it, she assumed he would force her head into the window to scream in her ear which had become normal practice if he wanted to question her after a shift and she provided a 'smart arse' or insufficient answer.

His eyes had been soft and his teeth weren't gritted as he reached out but Teeny's body had already reacted, making the decision for her.

"Nut, fuck off! Don't fucking touch me!" she screamed slapping his arm away and he awkwardly tried to get a hold of her face to look at her and speak to her but she frantically squealed and screamed and threw her arms around so he couldn't quite get a grip of her.

"Get the fuck off of me!" she continued and flicked her seatbelt off and pushed all her weight into the door and as she opened the car door, fell on her back onto the cold, frosted road.

"Colette! fuck sake, come here!" Mark shouted, exasperated, taking off his own seatbelt and trying to come around to help Teeny off of the deck.

She pulled herself up quickly and tried to get away from him as he lurched towards her from the rear end of the car. She scrambled towards the front of the car before he wrestled her into submission, both of them leaning over the bonnet, her face on the cold metal, him over her holding her arms down, both their breaths billowing clouds into the cold night. The whole scene lit up like a drive thru film with his headlights still on. Teeny continued to wriggle.

"Whit the fuck are you doing, stop! Stay still, you crazy bitch," Mark seethed through his teeth trying to tame the wild, wounded animal she was becoming, trying to thrash away from him.

He was too powerful for her. He continued to hold her as she stopped thrashing and began to whimper her defeat.

"I wasn't going to hit you, I'm *not* going to hurt you, OK? I'm going to let go, I just want to talk."

He slowly released her and stood up backing gently away from the car to give Teeny room to stand up and face him. Her mind was reeling, this scene was like something from a bad soap. He'd only ever hit her in the car or in his flat and he was normally so direct about it. This torment was new. Why drive her somewhere first, was he going to kill her this time?

She spun around to face him. "Then why are we here, if you 'just want to talk', why didn't we go home? Did you want to throw me in the canal afterwards?"

Mark scanned the setting quickly and made the connection Teeny was trying to toss together in her frantic, inebriated state.

"Jesus fucking Christ, Colette, don't be dramatic!" he answered, seeming genuinely appalled with her assumption. "I-I just…" he started but trailed off.

He turned away from the glaring spotlight of the headlights and rubbed his head, mumbling something inaudible.

Teeny stood waiting for him to explain. When he turned around, he had tears in his eyes and the tip of his nose was pink with the cold.

"I was so fucking angry, Colette. I knew if we went home, I'd have hurt you. That's why I just kept driving. I couldn't take my hands off the wheel 'cause I just wanted to…" He balled up his fist and licked his lips as he looked for the right words to use.

Teeny felt sick and her nerves and the wintery night made her chitter. "You've barely moved for three weeks, cried constantly, looked like shit then it's as if you pick an argument with me so you can fuck off out with him and Ashley all dolled up just to give two fingers up to me? That's a dirty move. Then when I come to speak to you, you're wrecked and letting some stranger feel you up in a bus stop! Whit the fuck am I meant to think?"

This jigsaw piece could not fit into Teeny's mind. That wasn't her intention, she thought she was just doing something fun for herself, was she being malicious? Was there a spiteful undertone of her movements to hurt Mark for being a shit earlier? Maybe she was punishing him for giving up on the counselling after one session. Too cold to think properly or articulate a reasonable counter argument, her jaws ached from chittering and her lower back was sore from the fall from the car, she started to cry again. She felt so ridiculous for assuming the worst and behaving like a child in the car. She was embarrassed for herself for thrashing around like an injured animal and all he wanted to do was talk to her.

"I'm sorry," was all she could manage. "I don't, I'm-I'm sorry?" Confused and cold, she continued to sob, rubbing her arms and Mark took his own coat off and put it around her shoulders.

"Shit, you must be freezing. Come on, get in the car."

She rubbed her hands along the grated fans to feel the heat blow and thaw her fingers and rubbed her cheek against the hard-wool collar of his coat. It was comforting though raw and scratchy at her tender, cold face. She could smell him and his aftershave and feel his warmth at the same time as feel the nipping fabric on her skin.

She watched the kettle boil as Mark set up cups and poured her tea. She didn't comment on there being no sugar added. She held the cup for a long time and breathed the steam in through her nose to attempt to defrost her frozen thoughts. It was one in the morning now and Mark would be getting up early for work. Teeny felt guilty for keeping him up so late when he told her he had work and to specifically not be late.

"Do you want to go to bed, I'll clear up here?" she offered as she took in the scenes in the lounge. The smashed glass on the floor, the toppled candles and plants, soil spilled over the rug. This would be the aftermath from her hanging up the phone on him earlier.

"No, leave it. I'll sort it when I get back in tomorrow. I think we need to talk more about what happened though?" he added.

She agreed but she was exhausted now. It had seemed like days ago she was sitting nervously bouncing her leg in the doctor's waiting room. Her eyes dipped and her weight felt heavy on her forearms as she slouched over the breakfast bar.

"Right. Bed," Mark ordered sliding the hot cup away so she wouldn't get scalded but allowed himself a small laugh at her sleepy state.

She slept soundly enough but her full bladder pushed her out of bed around 6:30 am. She tiptoed in the dark into the en suite leaving the light off. She felt around in the dark for some make up wipes to clear away the eyeliner that was now smeared over her nose and stinging her eyes. She quickly brushed her teeth too and slurped at the tap for a drink to save going through to the kitchen. The heating wouldn't come on until 7 and the bathroom was freezing. She hurried back into bed and tried to warm herself back up to nod off but her brain had already clocked in for the early shift and was replaying the previous 24 hours to her in a loop.

The doctor, Chloe, the baby, Ryan, Mark, college, the counsellor, Mark, Mark's parents, Ashley, Michael, Mark, the bus stop, Mark, the canal, the cold, Mark. A part of her was relieved when he showed up to collect her last night. She was grateful even. She had drunk too much and didn't have the words to deal with the romantic invasion pawing onto her. It troubled her how he found her though. She didn't say where she was meeting Ashley and he wouldn't have been able to read her phone before she went out. She wondered if perhaps someone had shouted something in the background when she was on the phone that might clue him in or had he followed her and been outside the whole night watching? Her movements in the bed and cold skin had roused Mark and he turned around to shape himself against her, nuzzling into her hair and holding her hip.

"You alright?" he asked sleepily.

Teeny knew if she didn't ask the question now, the words would have dragged themselves through her mind all day taking over her brain like weeds.

"How did you know where to find me? Last night. I didn't say where I was." She stopped herself from throwing her own theories to give him ideas and let him answer instead.

He exhaled sharply in frustration then lay on his back, roughly rearranging the quilt. She could hear him checking his phone on the bedside table for the time.

"This is ridiculous, go to sleep, I need to get ready for work soon."

Teeny shuffled onto her other side so she could face him. "Why is it ridiculous? I'm just asking how you knew exactly where to come and get me?"

He looked at her for a long time, she had propped herself up on her elbow now and her eyes were wide and searching.

"I tracked your phone. The 'find my iPhone' thing, I used that," he answered quietly but not guiltily.

Teeny stared back at him unable to disguise her shock and anger. She lay back on the pillow and laughed in disbelief.

"I only did it to keep you safe. Fuck knows what you were up to out there with that smug prick and you were adamant you weren't coming home so I was coming to find you to come speak to me. Maybe if you had told me where you were going in the first place and who with, I wouldn't have needed to? Lucky I fucking did or you'd probably be waking up in his bed this morning or your new pal from the bus stop or fuck, maybe both of them, eh?" he shouted defensively.

He had pulled himself up to sitting position and was shaking his head at her waiting for her reaction.

Almost instinctively, she pulled herself up, climbing into his lap with her legs wrapped around his back and pulling the quilt around them with her arms around his shoulders.

"This is the only bed I want to wake up in, Mark. With you. There is nothing going on between Michael and I and I really didn't know he was coming out when I made the plans with Ashley, but he is my friend." She kissed him softly on the lips so he would look at her. "You don't have to come hunting for me though, that's really not necessary and a little fucking weird, let's be honest?" she said with a reasoning tone, aware she was pushing her luck and his temper but remembered his words from the night before, *I'm not going to hurt you.*

He looked away and released his hands which had been clasped at the small of her back.

"I haven't been unfaithful to you and I won't be." She tried to reassure him putting her head against his.

"I just don't see why he still needs to be in your life. You're not in college anymore. What other reason could you have for him hanging about?" he said finally pulling back to look at her.

Teeny didn't have an answer. She'd felt the chasm between the three of them last night but didn't think that meant she would need to cut them off as friends, maybe their friendship would just look slightly different now. At the same time, she didn't want to feel the anxiety and stress every time she was in his company for fear of how Mark would react. Was she really that close to Michael anyway? She would need to think about having to navigate her friendship with Ashley

125

as a twosome but she would. She would do it for him so he could relax and begin to trust her. She realised this was a cross she would need to bear, a cross she put on her own shoulders that first night she kissed Mark when Ryan was asleep in their bed. She had been a cheat, a reputation that would be hard to shake even when she was still with the man she cheated with. The 'scarlet A' burning into her flesh, a constant reminder who she was now and what she was capable of.

"I won't see him anymore. I won't. You're more important to me and I don't want you worrying that I'm looking for someone else every time I leave the house."

This seemed to appease him. He reached his arms under her t-shirt and softly drew lines down her spine while resting his head against her chest. They sat listening to each other's breathing and heartbeats and the spell was broken with Mark's 7 am alarm.

"I need to get in the shower," he said as he pushed Teeny back onto her pillow, kissing her and playfully throwing the quilt over her face. She smiled, feeling a sense of peace had been restored that she had a plan on how to get her relationship back on track and be the good person, or 'good girl' she liked to imagine herself as. She wanted to hold onto this feeling where there no angst or heavy silences or tense atmosphere.

Normally, Teeny would force herself to sleep until as late as possible so she would have less hours to contend by herself if she didn't have a shift in the pub. Today, she felt energised and focussed and was afraid to fall back asleep in case she was actually still drunk and falling back asleep would guarantee a hangover later in the morning. She pulled on her joggers and a housecoat, the flat still only warming up and still so dark outside. She made herself useful by attempting to make a pot of coffee which Mark would usually do after his shower. After listening in and confirming that Mark was still in the bathroom, Teeny set about sweeping up the glass and soil. Too early to hoover. She could imagine his rage as he threw his glass and kicked or pushed the planter over, closing her eyes tightly to push away the unpleasant vision.

"I thought you'd have dozed back off by now?" Mark commented as he entered the lounge buttoning the cuffs of his shirt.

"Well, I'm up now so thought I'd just stay up." She smiled, handing him his cup.

After he left for the train, she decided to check the financial damage she'd caused last night. Teeny would no longer receive any bursaries or grants she depended on to make a suitable income, so now lived solely off her pittance wages from the pub, rent free, in Mark's flat. She couldn't really afford to have reckless nights in the pub with her friends anymore. Pulling her make-up and keys aside, she remembered her prescription and hurriedly took her pill while it was on her mind. At least they'd be able to stop using condoms now which had been a nuisance and a turn off for Mark. It boosted her knowing that she could please him properly and he wouldn't have to pull a face of contempt each time she reminded him she still needed a new prescription. There were still some notes left in her purse, so not all bad, and next to them, the two information cards given to her by Dr Donaldson the day before.

Out of curiosity, Teeny googled one of the sites on her phone and clicked through a couple of the pages. It struck her how familiar the bullet points of symptoms were. Some of them dating further back to before her pill ran out. Before Mark had become violent towards her. Her rage, her attacks of being unable to feel where she was, losing reality, losing time, her lack of concentration, her inability to enjoy things. She'd noticed these things before, not all the time but they had definitely played their part in her life over the last couple of years. 'Pharmaceutical Remedies'. She scrolled immediately past the heading and then anything with pills or tablets or medicine mentioned in it. Teeny didn't necessarily think it was 'depression and/or anxiety' she had, like the doctor had alluded to, like her mother. She would refuse to take medicine for it even if that turned out to be the case. She wouldn't live under the sickly thick fog of indifference her mother had become so accustomed to.

She continued to scroll and click on some of the self-help methods. Exercise. Breathing. A balanced diet. Teeny rolled her eyes, *That simple, eh?* Rubbing her tender back, she sipped her coffee which was now cold. It was getting slightly lighter outside and she moved over to the bay window. She watched as the early birds huddled into themselves trying to keep warm and get quickly out of the cold, throwing up shutters and putting sandwich boards outside their shops.

Fuck it, it can't hurt, she thought as she decided to take some control over her mind and while away some of the hours of the day by going for a walk.

11. 8 December 2018

"They've got cars big as bars, they've got rivers of gold…" Teeny half-sang, half-hummed along to the radio while looking for a lint roller or maybe some Sellotape. She wanted to look her best tonight. Mark had invited her along to his company's Christmas party but she got the impression he was hoping she would decline. Was he ashamed of her? Was he hiding an office romance? Her interest peaked and she wanted to make sure she looked the part; someone he'd be proud to have on his arm.

She realised she knew and saw so little of his life outside of their little bubble. Deek was more of 'an acquaintance from the pub' as Mark described and he didn't really talk of other friends or 'work buddies'. It would be good for them to go out and enjoy themselves, soak up the Christmas spirit. Lights and music were everywhere and it had been such a long time since they went out together. She was excited. She chose a high-necked black cocktail dress to avoid any accusations that she was purposely 'flashing her tits to everyone' with multi-coloured jewels over the neckline for a festive touch. Giving up on the lint roller, she grabbed some Sellotape and folded some in half to lift off some lint to keep the dress perfect as it hung on the door. She sat at the breakfast bar in her housecoat to dry her hair since Mark hated it when she dried her hair in the same room as him and he was already in there ironing. As the room began to warm up with the heat from the hair dryer, she shuffled out of the housecoat and allowed it to drape around her waist while she straightened her hair and put some make up on.

"Christ, I hope you're wearing more than that?" Mark commented jokingly as he walked into the lounge to a topless Teeny at the breakfast bar.

She smiled shyly in return, stifling the joke she wanted to make in case it triggered a nippy response. As she wrapped up the cord on her straighteners, she stepped off of the stool attempting to catch the falling housecoat and failed. When she rose back up from picking it up, Mark was behind her, holding her wrist tight so she would drop the housecoat, his other hand skimming over her breasts and between her legs. As he guided her to lean over the breakfast bar she protested, "Och, dinnae, I've just done my hair, I'll get all sweaty."

He didn't release his grip of her wrist, only placing it on the bar so she could support herself.

"So? It's only me that should be looking anyway. Unless there's someone else you're dressing up for?"

Instead of answering, she sighed her defeat, pushing herself back toward him, an offering of peacekeeping. Teeny watched them move in the window reflection against the early evening dark sky, she forced herself to look away, slightly disgusted with herself. An all too familiar wisp of shame creeping into her mind of hands from behind, on her, confusing her of what was happening. She let out a whimpering moan to pull away from the assaulting, clouded memory but Mark only assumed she was enjoying his act of spontaneity. He gripped the skin on her hips as he came, making her wince slightly and walked back towards the bathroom advising her he was heading for his shower and she should make sure she was ready in 20 minutes. She lifted the housecoat again, wrapping it around her like a towel while looking at her dress. She shook her head and turned to clear away her make-up, catching sight of herself in her compact mirror she had been using. She slammed it shut and tossed it in the bag along with the other stage pieces lying around and slid the whole bag along the bar letting it fall and clatter to the ground. Teeny quickly glanced around the bar to make sure she hadn't made any mess with her little tantrum then went through to the bedroom to finish getting ready.

They made their way towards the turnstiles with Mark roughly tugging at Teeny's arm as she struggled with her high heels. Having lived in bare feet and trainers or boots for the last couple of months, she was a little rusty.

"Will you hurry the fuck up; it's packed in here!" He griped in frustration as she tried to keep up to avoid the queue of party goers and commuters at the gates.

She felt heat in her neck, embarrassed if anyone was watching her getting 'a row'. She bit her lip not letting her embarrassment turn to tears and tried to concentrate on her feet. They stepped out into the rainy evening. Luckily, the hotel where they were headed was only a five-minute walk away from Queen Street. Upon their entry, it was as if a button had been pressed on Mark's back in the hotel reception; he switched to the calm, charming prince she'd fallen in love with. He helped her out of her coat and took her umbrella, letting Teeny arrange her dress and fix her hair.

"Gorgeous," he commented, kissing her sweetly on the lips, careful not to smear her lipstick. Teeny felt butterflies in her stomach as he led her through to a function suite where the music was loud and the atmosphere was merry. Mark quickly spotted his colleagues and they walked over to greet them. They had all enthusiastically shaken her hand or kissed and hugged her but Teeny couldn't miss the raised eyebrows his male colleagues gave Mark when they took her in, appraising her. She drank the prosecco that was available on the table, not her usual taste but she felt it made her look more sophisticated, more mature with this crowd. Drinking in the company of people older than her was not a new experience. In fact, this lot were pretty on par with the standard Saturday night regulars in the Cross Keys. This was somehow different though. Their experience, class and general air seemed to outweigh Teeny's as well as their years.

On her third glass of nervously over sipping, Mark slipped his hand around her waist to take the empty glass out of her hand and whispered, "Slow. Down," in her ear before giving her a tight smile as he pulled back to re-join the conversation.

She nodded and excused herself to go to the bathroom to try to sober up, feeling the fizz warm her face and make her heels even more unmanageable. She sat in the cubicle taking in some deep breaths like she had been practicing at home and feeling the fabric on her dress to ground her. She leaned forward with her elbows on her knees and her face on her hands to try to steady her nerves. She had heard other women at the sinks discussing where they had bought their dresses and the colour of their acrylics but had been tuning them out to concentrate.

"Did you see the wee young thing Mark brought in?" one commented and Teeny sat fully up to listen.

"Fuck off! Is that his girlfriend? I thought she was a wee new start and he had just happened to walk in with her?" the other answered.

"Newstart? Fi the fucking school training scheme like? She looks about 18!" The women giggled and continued to sort their make-up and respray their hair. Teeny dusted herself off and was ready to walk assertively out to the sinks to show them she had been listening to make them feel like shit but she couldn't trust herself to. She knew she would end up crying or having a screaming fit and only proving herself to be the child they were describing.

"I always thought he was gay, to be honest, he was always that polite wey and never tried it on like the rest of them," the first woman continued.

"Naw, mind he went out with, och what's her name again? She worked the floor upstairs, in Danny's team? Fuck, her name has disappeared but they went out for a good couple of years then she went back to her folks in Ireland to live," the second woman explained, not realising she was giving Teeny the first insight she'd ever heard of Mark having any kind of ex.

"I take it she was too old for him?" the first woman responded and they both cackled as they clicked their heels out of the bathroom leaving Teeny with her hands against the cubicle door.

She slowly returned to the table and checked her phone knowing there wouldn't be any messages or missed calls but wanted to have some kind of prop in her hand that wasn't a drink. Mark was deep in conversation and hadn't noticed her standing awkwardly behind the group.

"Colette, is it?" one of the women asked and gestured to Teeny that she should join them for a dance. She glanced over to Mark and he smiled at her signalling she had permission to go and dance. Teeny didn't recognise her voice from the toilet and she seemed a little younger than those other women so felt comfortable enough joining her and a couple of the team on the dancefloor. Her name was Sarah and she didn't work with Mark but her husband did and this night out wasn't her first rodeo so she took Teeny under her wing for some company. They awkwardly shoe shuffled to some kind of Christmas medley and some pop classics while making small talk.

"They'll be yappin' aw night, I just leave them to it," Sarah explained.

Teeny smiled politely, only really catching half of what she said over the music, but got the gist. Sarah guided her to the bar and ordered them both drinks so they could rest their feet, she explained that another hour or so and she'd be dancing in her bare feet.

Even the posh lassies take their shoes off for a dance, Teeny thought and smiled to herself.

"So how long have you and Mark been together?" she asked as they found a small, quieter table just off the bar area.

"About seven or eight months," Teeny confirmed.

"Ah, so still in the honeymoon phase? Christ, that was the best part, the first bit. Can't stop blethering, can't stop thinking of them, can't stop…eh, keeping your hands off each other!" she finished, laughing, realising she might be oversharing with Teeny, a stranger and quite a young woman.

Teeny still giggled nervously to show she understood. It seemed though that that phase was over a long time ago. When did it get so serious? She was so rarely asked how long she and Mark had been together that it struck her it had still only been under a year. They hadn't had an anniversary; they hadn't had a Christmas or a Valentine's together or even his birthday. It all seemed so long ago that she first saw him and couldn't keep her eyes off of him but in reality, wasn't very long ago at all. Sarah and her husband, Mick, had been married for ten years with two young kids. She worked in IT and Teeny couldn't help but get the impression that her husband's Christmas party was the big social event of her year. She almost felt sorry for her but then she looked so happy, as if she was genuinely enjoying her night, the company and the freedom away from the kids maybe.

Teeny wondered if life was much simpler and happier the less you asked of it, just to go with the flow and not worry so much and think so much. As she pondered to the soundtrack of Sarah telling a story of one of her kids swearing in the supermarket, Mark appeared in the corner of her eye. He had power walked through the double doors as if on the rampage but caught his slipping mask of charm when he saw Teeny, alone, sitting talking to Sarah.

"I hope you're not stealing her the full night, I'm after a dance," he teased, coming up to stand behind Sarah. They went back into the main room with their drinks and Mark took Teeny up to the dancefloor to what sounded like the third time Ed Sheeran had played for the night. He nuzzled into her neck as they danced slowly.

"Are you having a good time? What was Sarah saying to it?" he quizzed.

"Not much. Usual stuff. So, who's the ex you worked with?" She tried to sound innocently curious rather than annoyed and pulled back from their embrace to raise her eyebrows at him.

"What did she say about her like? Why the fuck would you two be talking about her?" he answered sharply and defensively. They had come to a halt but were still in their dance pose.

"We weren't. I overheard a couple of women talking about an ex of yours from the company while slagging your 'child bride'? While I was sitting in the toilet like a tit," she answered in a self-mocking tone trying to turn the cackling witches from the bathroom into the enemy to take the heat off of herself. Teeny continued, "Anyway, why didn't you say you had an ex? You said you'd 'never been with anyone of importance'. A couple of years with someone sounds 'of importance' to me?"

"Why the fuck does it matter? She doesn't even live in the country anymore so don't start. Jealousy isn't a pretty colour on you," he answered with contempt for her even raising it. Teeny couldn't help but scoff.

"Me, jealous? That's fucking rich!" she shouted a little louder than she meant or was necessary but anger boiled in her chest and she had tried to shake out of the dance hold but Mark stood firm holding her. He looked around to make sure his colleagues hadn't clocked their little scene and gave her a warning glare to behave. She shrugged out of his arms and walked back towards the table and helped herself to another glass of prosecco which had appeared next to her handbag. For the next couple of hours, she clung to Sarah so that Mark couldn't have her on his own. She danced more than she

136

normally cared for but the bubbles of the alcohol swam to her head and she kicked her heels off and laughed while attempting to do the Slosh with a very seasoned dancer in Sarah.

As the evening dwindled down, Mark brought Teeny her coat which she took without a word to him and put it on, swapping numbers with Sarah knowing they would not keep in contact. She stepped back into her heels and kissed and hugged her, wishing them and the kids a Merry Christmas when it came. Mark made pleasantries with some of the other people from the team and Teeny walked through the hotel reception with him behind her out into the cold, wet night.

"Enough, Colette. Give it a fucking rest," Mark warned as Teeny marched through the flat in silence having studiously ignored him the entire journey home. She felt safe enough with there being so many people around and had time to let her rage seep in. She pulled her earrings out and threw them haphazardly on top of the drawers letting one of them slide to the floor. She kicked her shoes off tossing them into the wardrobe. She stood in her bare feet flexing her toes into the carpet feeling the material soothe her aching feet from wearing the heels. She realised she looked ridiculous but she didn't know how to challenge him properly, how to discuss the matter further without it deteriorating into a screaming match and she deeply resented his accusation of him calling her jealous. It hadn't occurred to Teeny to feel jealous until now but she'd had the entire train journey to imagine all sorts of scenarios. 'Was she "the one that got away"?' 'Did she break his heart?' 'Did she look like her?' 'Had he hit her too?'

"It's a simple question, Mark, what was her name?" She waited with her hands on her hips.

He shook his head and breathed out a long sigh through his nose. "Lauren. Her name was Lauren. We dated for about two years. Never lived together. She got a post with the branch in Dublin so moved back home with her parents. The end. That's it," he answered with frustrating finality.

"No, that's not it. Why would you never mention her, not even vaguely? Why hide her? You know absolutely everything about me including everyone I've slept with and you don't even think to mention someone you went out with for two fucking years?" she screamed angrily.

"Lower your fucking voice, you're acting like a child," he snarled back.

"Aw, fuck you, Mark. Fuck you," she shouted, having no proper response. She felt defenceless and allowed herself to act on impulses that she buried down all too often.

As she pushed past him at the doorway, he grabbed her by the straps of the dress pushing her back against the drawers. She pulled frantically at his hands and slapped at his shoulders to get him off. He put both hands around her neck choking her and wrestling her to the floor as he did.

"ENOUGH! You're acting like a fucking brat. Keep fucking going, Colette, Keep going!" he challenged as he shouted louder in her ear, taking one of his hands off and balled it up in a fist next to her face. Teeny looked at him and for the first time felt hate and disdain towards him. In previous times when he had hurt her or threatened to, she had felt fear or overwhelming sadness and just wanted him to quieten down and be normal with her again. Tonight, she saw him for a man, not a prince with anger management issues. She imagined him in the pub as another punter, someone who had come the cunt after being put out and she was ready for the fight. She drew her knee up hard between his legs and he collapsed, rolling off of her in agony. She quickly got up onto her knees punching and kneeing his back as he rolled clinging to his aching balls. Being as slight as she was, there was probably little impact of her blows but she realised she was no better than him so stopped herself. She stood up rubbing her neck and trying to get her breath back and reality shattered around her ears. He was stronger than her, he could really hurt her.

She hurriedly walked into the hall grabbing his gym trainers that were sitting and ran out the door trying to ignore him swearing and screaming her name as she let the door slam behind her. She stepped into his oversized trainers and ran down the stairs and outside and practically ran into someone hunched down outside the door, smoking. She tumbled over them to avoid stepping on them, scraping her knee and her dress coming up past her hips as she did so.

"Shit, I'm sorry, are you OK?" the English accent beside her asked.

"Whit the fuck! Who the fuck sits right at the fucking close door?" Teeny screamed frantically.

The strange woman held her hands up in fright or defence, she wasn't sure but Teeny could hear Mark coming out the flat door and she panicked. "Please, I'm not here, OK? I'm not here," Teeny pleaded as she ran around the corner towards the bin store.

As soon as she was out of sight, Mark came out of the door and a little startled at the strange woman still holding her hands up. "Eh, have you seen a young woman come out here just a minute ago? Which way did she go?" he asked as calmly as he could.

"She sprinted across the car park, that way," she said, pointing in the opposite direction of where Teeny had hid. He thanked her and walked briskly across the car park with a strange limp.

Teeny watched him walk towards the High Street and came back out to her accomplice. "Thanks. I wasn't ready to go back in yet," she offered, embarrassed at the scene and wincing at her poor scraped knee.

"Yeh, I figured. The trainers are a bit of a giveaway, you want some?" she said exhaling her smoke and offering Teeny the joint. She shook her head but took up the offer of a wet cloth for her knee.

"I'm Jen, by the way, sorry for killing your getaway. Rough night?" she asked as they took a seat in Jen's flat on the ground floor.

"Colette," she said, accepting the cloth and slowly patting it over her nipping knee and shin.

"It's OK, I don't think I would have gotten far without him seeing me across the car park," she continued.

Jen looked at her awkwardly, unsure if she should probe further. Unsure if she wanted the hassle or the unwelcome drama.

"Are you OK though, yeh? I've…I've heard him do a fair bit of shouting," she said explaining that despite living diagonally opposite them within the block, she enjoyed taking her smoke outside and would often hear them arguing if the bedroom window was open.

Teeny was mortified, her instincts wanted to shout at her for being a nosy cow but then she remembered she'd literally fallen into her lap running away from him so defending their relationship was somewhat moot at this point.

"I'm OK. He's just loud when he's angry sometimes," she confirmed.

Jen looked doubtful at her minimising of the situation but didn't want to press harder right now. She made them both tea and Teeny looked around the flat which was a little smaller than Mark's and covered in art; paintings, photographs, tapestries. There was so much colour and so many strong smells between the incense burning, the wax melts, whatever was in the slow cooker and the overpowering smell of weed coming from Jen herself.

"So, are you an artist or something?" Teeny tried for small talk.

"Uh, or something," Jen laughed. "I dabble in a bit of all sorts but I like to paint," she explained.

"So, is that what you do, do you like, sell it?" Teeny continued, she knew nothing about art herself but there were pictures of red and purple cacti, they looked kind of shitty and poorly done.

"Oh fuck no, nah just for fun, for the soul, you know? I teach yoga and Pilates, that's where the money is now," she elaborated flexing her eyebrows.

"That's pretty cool," Teeny responded aware her tone sounded sarcastic but she meant it quite sincerely. "Stretching for money and painting for fun," she accidentally said aloud.

Jen laughed and responded before Teeny had a chance to apologise and correct herself.

"Well yes, a toddler's dream is my reality I suppose," she said in a reflecting tone and the women laughed then sipped from their cups.

Teeny noted that Jen could only be in her early thirties but seemed much older, living her life as if she had retired

141

already. She felt a pang of real jealousy of this easy, colourful lifestyle she had immersed herself in. The women talked about music and local restaurants; Jen, taken by surprise at how similar their music tastes were. She had been letting her guest listen to different clips on YouTube of covers of songs she liked when she noticed that Teeny had become withdrawn and distracted.

"I think he's back home, I just heard the main door bang," Teeny said continuing to listen for the confirmation of footsteps going up the stairs and the keys going in the door. "I better go back up, I suppose," she added after a minute or so of silence and the two women looking towards the ceiling.

"You don't have to. Look, I know it's none of my business but Colette, he doesn't seem like a very nice guy. You're welcome to kip here tonight if you don't want to go back up there?" Jen offered.

Teeny considered the offer but knew it would be easier to go home sooner rather than later and check the lie of the land.

"No, it's fine, honestly, I'll just go up there now," she said as she got up from the sofa and placed her cup next to the sink.

"Well, come back down tomorrow, yeh? We can get a proper chat when you're not in your party dress and I'm not in my PJ's?" Jen laughed.

"Yeh, that sounds good, maybe you can teach me some yoga?" Teeny laughed and did her best namaste stance.

She thanked her neighbour for her impromptu hospitality and lifted Mark's shoes from the hall as she wandered up the stairs and knocked on the door having left too quickly to lift keys of her own.

Mark answered the door warily and when he realised it was Teeny at the door and not the police, looked

142

tremendously relieved. He stepped aside, letting her walk through the flat. She noted on the sofa that her phone lay out next to his, which had previously been in her handbag. This no longer bothered her, she mostly used it to call Darren for her shifts or Mark now anyway. She stopped at the entrance to the lounge, "I'm going to bed." She sighed.

"Look, I'm really sorry, sweetheart. I just got caught up there but I didn't hit you. And if anything, I should be raging with you – you could have fucking paralysed me with that move. You can ask me about Lauren, what do you want to know? I'll talk about her, honestly, what do you want to know?" he almost pleaded with a hint of desperation in his voice.

She wanted to say 'No, goodnight'. She wanted to layer it with thick apathy to express her derision with him. Her contempt of him. But she also wanted to know if she was so special after all.

"Did you ever lift your hands to her?" she asked quietly.

Not what Mark had expected her to ask. He looked shocked and then edgy, his eyes looking to the sides and the floor for the answer to the question only he could really have.

"I'm not a psychopath, Colette, I'm not out there battering women, putting them in hospital. I've just got trouble with my temper sometimes," he said finally.

"That's not what I asked," she continued as she walked into the bedroom changing into her t-shirt while simultaneously taking off her make-up.

She realised that she probably already knew the answer. Mark would tell her whichever version suited his narrative best and put him in the best light. So, Lauren moved back to

143

Ireland for a shiny new job and to live with her parents, not to escape an abusive, controlling partner.

She crawled over the bed to her side to flick on the bedside lamp then walked up to him still in the doorway to turn off the main light, leaving them in the dark while the lamp powered up. She lay in bed on her side facing the window, away from him, with the quilt pulled up under her chin. She thought about how pathetic and sad he looked standing there and she could still hear him breathing, watching her. A twisted part of her wanted him to slide under the covers behind her, holding her close to him and tell her whatever she needed to hear to not feel like this. The anger, the shame, the toll of it all was becoming exhausting. She sniffed quietly, allowing the tears to fall down her face and soak into the pillow. She could hear him undress then turn off the other lights in the flat before coming to bed. He walked around and crouched down so he sat on his knees facing her. He whispered in her ear of how much he loved her, how he was sorry and told her not to cry as he tucked her hair behind her ear so he could see her face and kiss her cheek, tasting her tears. She knew something irreparable was broken tonight but still wanted to hold him, feel his warmth and the weight of him surrounding her, making her feel secure. She reached up still with her eyes closed and swept his hair and touched his face stroking his lip. As he kissed her fingers, he lifted the quilt to lay closer to her, his skin was cold but Teeny could feel his heart beating against her chest as he lay on top of her.

"Did I hurt you?" Teeny murmured in between kisses while skimming the band on his boxers.

"Mmm hmm. Enough to probably stop me having kids but not enough to discourage me," he answered, laughing slightly while kissing her tender neck and helping her wriggle out of her underwear. He propped himself up on his elbow so he could watch her face as he touched her and she writhed towards his hand.

"Lie still," he whispered and she complied trying to stay in this moment and not let her thoughts become overly clear. Her mind trailed off to the Christmas party, the women in the bathroom, Sarah, the prosecco, Lauren, the train journey home, his hands on her dress, the weight of him on her when he choked her, Jen, the smell of weed. She scrambled to come back to the present and he kissed and stroked her until her body gave over to the sensations and her back arched and his kiss was on her mouth to absorb her orgasm. He held her head covering her ears and she helped him ease into her. She wrapped her legs around his waist and they kissed slowly and gently. Afterward, he lay on her chest listening to her breathing, both needing to get up but neither wanting to bring the feeling to an end. Teeny knew eventually she would need to get up, go to the bathroom and look at herself in the mirror, work out who the fuck she was and what she was doing with her life. But for tonight, they would lie in their mixed sweat and synced pulses for as long as possible.

12. 18 December 2018

"How long do I sit like this?" Teeny asked starting to feel self-conscious and ridiculous. "I've got a shift at three o'clock, mind?" she continued, laughing.

"OK, when you breathe out this time, you can pull yourself back up then go into child's pose," Jen relieved Teeny of her stance. "Yep, on your knees like that and yeh, hands like that," she continued, gently talking her into the pose.

Teeny had nervously knocked on Jen's door as soon as Mark had left for work that Monday after the Christmas party. More so to apologise for the chaos she literally threw into her lap while she was simply out trying to relax. She knew the longer she left the conversation, the more anxious it would make her and she felt she was just starting to get a handle on the panic attacks.

She'd spent most mornings with her since that Monday, seen as the majority of Jen's classes were in the afternoon and evening. Teeny cursed herself for joking about the yoga as Jen was now trying to get her to fold herself into a pretzel. She found that, with Jen and within a very short space of time, she was sharing so many pieces of herself, unprompted and not asked for. Jen had such an inviting, relaxing presence that she couldn't help but wear her heart on her sleeve. Other than talking about Mark. This topic had not been raised again as it seemed to already go without saying he was abusive and violent. Teeny couldn't be sure how much she had heard or knew and didn't want to confirm or have to deny so thought it best just not to mention him. They had so many other things to talk about despite him. Jen had recommended Teeny take up more yoga and look into 'mindfulness' to help with the anxiety. She agreed with Teeny about avoiding the anti-depressants since they 'turned you into a zombie'.

"I'll stick to my own drugs, thank you very much." She signalled to the joint she was rolling then excused herself go outside for a smoke.

Teeny joined her outside but still refused any, the smell turned her stomach. After a few minutes, Jen looked at Teeny and tried to say as casually as possible, "Your body carries trauma, you know. I know it sounds kinda 'woo woo' but it does. We learned about it when I did my instructors course. It's all to do with where you carry your energy like, for example, someone who had maybe been raped years ago might fucking kick off trying to do the 'happy baby' pose because it triggers their body's memories even if they hadn't even been thinking about it. Fucking mad stuff how the body and mind work, mate."

Teeny nodded and looked away. The 'downward dog' pose had made her feel sick and shameful. Jen stood aside her with her hands gently hovering, not really touching her to instruct her on how to better hold the pose to loosen up and stretch out. Teeny hated that she couldn't see her but knew her hands were on her. The images flashed in her mind; the yellow dress, the stack of coins, hands. She had wanted to hit

147

her, to instinctively reach her hand out and swipe behind her knees so that she'd fall on her arse. Her anger and fear had caught her off guard and she felt guilty for thinking like that of her new friend who was only doing what she knew how to do best.

"Mad stuff," she echoed Jen's comment.

"Why do you still work in that place if you need to see those creeps every time? That would totally freak me out." Jen continued feeling she'd successfully opened the door.

"'Cause maybe I dreamt it or imagined it, I can't actually remember them doing anything and I certainly couldn't double-check with them or throw a drink in their face, 'just in case they did', I'd be locked up," Teeny responded, feeling very defensive and conscious she had overshared some of her troubled memories with Jen who'd she'd only met a couple of weeks ago.

"Maybe so, but that doesn't mean you have to stick around them either. Listen to what your body is telling you. Between your dad being your best customer and those two making your skin crawl…why not run in the opposite direction, babe?" Jen asked so sincerely.

Teeny didn't have an answer. The possibilities should be endless for her now that she wasn't studying accounting anymore which she hated anyway. She had no idea what else to do though, what else she would be good at. "I don't know, to be honest. What the fuck else is there to do?" she said finally after a long pause.

"Oh, please, Colette, you're a baby!" Catching Teeny's annoyed face, she continued, "I know, you hate the age thing but come on? You're 21! You've got years to figure this shit out. My advice would be ditching Mr Daddy Issues up the

148

stairs and see the world a bit, take the time to figure it out, figure you out?" Jen finished so sure of herself that she'd handed Teeny the magic prescription for all of her problems.

She hated the daddy issues comment, she could feel anger burning her face and neck but didn't want to shout or scream and lose her new friendship. It was nice to be able to speak with her and sit in her company and she never needed to explain herself to Mark because there was no trace of Jen on her phone, she only needed to knock the door.

"Hmm," was all she responded. "Well, for tonight, all I'm getting to see is the view from the bar, sounds like I'll need the wages to fund my trip around the world." She gave a sarcastic smile to Jen and headed back up the stairs to shower to get the smell off of her before her shift.

The pub had been busy enough for a Wednesday night, Teeny put it down to the Christmas spirit encouraging extra spends and jumping in the pub for a quick drink after a long day of Christmas shopping. Darren had hung around after his shift to have a couple of drinks and took his usual stool at the hatch. Teeny had been trying to help him with a crossword he was attempting but they were both as useless as each other and found the challenge of not relying on their phones for help difficult.

"Feat; take advantage of, seven letters? Any guesses, Teen?" Darren asked without lifting his head.

Teeny rested on her elbows thinking, refusing to check her phone and try to make her brain work.

"Seven letters," she thought aloud, "take advantage of," she continued as she served a couple of pints. Mark came through the door which wasn't like him; normally, he would text or phone and it had been a long time since a surprise visit from him would fill Teeny with a surge of excitement. The shock of seeing him unexpectedly did catch her off guard though. She wondered if she looked OK, was she maybe standing too close to anyone or smiling inappropriately?

"Exploit," she called over to Darren and answered Mark's knitted, confused face, "crossword. I didn't think you'd be in tonight?" she said, trying to keep her tone casual and not panicked.

"I feel like I haven't seen you for days with all the extra shifts you've been picking up," he answered Teeny but almost spoke directly to Darren who was sucking the scampi fries flavouring off his fingers before filling in the blank boxes in the crossword.

"Christmas time," Teeny offered as if this should be full explanation enough. "Gin?" she asked, reaching for the glass and ice at the same time.

Mark slipped slowly at his drink but continued to glance over to Darren. Teeny hated the look on his face. It was the face he'd have when he'd be brewing up for a night of accusations, gritted teeth and bruises. As she went to replace his drink, Mark hissed quietly, "Why the fuck is he still here anyway, I thought it was just you on tonight?"

Teeny bit her lip and mocked Darren saying, "'Cause he's no life and no pals so hangs around in here." She felt guilty for saying it but felt it put more distance between her and Mark's train of thought that he was hovering around the hatch for the same reason he himself did not so long ago.

As the hours ticked on, so did the amount of alcohol Mark put away. She didn't know how to cut him off. She wanted to be able to say, 'you're making me nervous. I'm frightened that you're getting angrier and more drunk and so more likely to hit me when I get home,' but she couldn't. So, she kept serving him. Thankfully, Darren left around 10:30 followed by the coffin dodgers and Auld Tam.

"Alone at last, eh?" Mark said with a snide-looking smile, the first time he'd smiled since coming in.

Teeny drew in her breath and continued emptying the dishwasher. She came around the other side to tidy the last couple of used tables, aware Mark was watching her every move.

"Do you remember the first time I fucked you? Right over there," he said, gesturing with his glass to the table where the coffin dodgers' imprints surely still sat.

Her stomach sank when she now made the connection. She hadn't at the time being too swept up in the passion of it all but now, looking back it seemed pretty seedy and fucked up for it to have been anywhere near that table.

Mark never spoke to her like this and it only heightened her anxiety. She blushed and nodded as she went to walk around him to check the kitchen. He swooped her into a clumsy embrace as she passed by and he kissed her greedily. She pulled away from his bitter kiss and tutted, muttering that she had to get sorted to lock up.

"What's the matter, sweetheart? You already had your fill before I came in?" he shouted after her as she stood in the kitchen rolling her eyes miming 'fuck off'.

"You're drunk, Mark, let's just get home, eh?" she shouted back, then, "Hopefully you'll fall asleep you slavering prick," more quietly to herself in the kitchen. Her shoulders tensed as she could hear him walk around into the kitchen. She met him at the doorway but he blocked her with one hand on her hip and one hand on the doorway.

"You used to love this. Me turning up and us at it all over the pub, what's changed?" He half sneered, already believing his own answer. "Is there someone else, you bored of me already? Already shagging someone else against the bandit, eh?" he finished as he shoved her roughly by the shoulders.

"Mark! Fuck sake! No! There is no one else, you're bloody hammered and I'm not in the fucking mood, awright?" Teeny shouted louder than her anxious state had wanted her to but her temper was bubbling over and taking control.

She'd had Jen's pearls of wisdom in her mind all day and had served in the shitty pub, served her drunk father and smelled the stale drink and piss all day. And now this. She'd hurt him before; she knew she could again if he forced her to it. Her shackles of fear transforming into something more tangible, weaponised, she felt her fists ball up in anticipation.

"Well, tell you what, sweetheart, how about you just close your eyes and imagine Darren and his crossword and that'll get you nice and wet, eh?" he'd mockingly breathed at her as he inched closer to her, cornering her into the wall.

"Mark, I swear, will you fuck off?" Teeny roared at him, shoving with all her weight but he was holding her tight by the shoulders. They banged and bashed into the soup pots stacked on the cooker and hadn't heard the creaky door and didn't notice Darren until he was at the back of Mark pulling him off by the coat.

"Get ti fuck, Mark, get out!" he shouted, pushing him towards the front door. Teeny's face flushed deep crimson as she tried to get her breath and step back out into the bar.

"Darren, please it's OK, I'm OK. Mark, go wait outside I'm just coming," she said, almost shrieked.

A shocked Darren was trying to get his bearings. "Nah, Teen, not OK, he had you in against the wa'. The fuck is happening here?"

Mark, still standing, snarling, trying to catch his own breath, hadn't said a word. Teeny took in the ridiculous scene, the two men stood in warrior poses, Darren's jacket and pizza box strewn on the floor.

"It's fine, I'm honestly, I'm fine," she started.

"What the fuck are you back for, anyway?" Mark finally said, breaking his seal of charm he'd managed to maintain here all these months.

"I forgot my fucking keys, you dick, what the fuck are you doing to Teeny?" he responded.

Teeny kicked herself mentally for not locking the door after they left. "We were just talking, fuck all to do with you," Mark stated, regaining some composure.

"Aye fucking looked like it right enough," Darren retorted sarcastically and Mark squared up against him, the two men within a breath away from each other.

"Mark, move," Teeny pleaded, pulling him backward. "Darren, please cash up. I'm sorry. I need to take him home. I'm sorry," she offered tearing up with embarrassment and guilt.

A look Darren had unfortunately seen before when Teeny had to bail in the middle of a shift to take her father home if he'd pissed himself or run home to her mother who'd casually phoned to tell her she'd taken all her pills at once. Darren, knowing he shouldn't be in charge of locking up since he'd been drinking, simply nodded once to Teeny then stared at

Mark and they never broke their mutual glare until Teeny had managed to yank him by the arm outside and pull the shutter down. She called the taxi and sat on the wall sobbing. "I can never show my face here again, I take it that's what you were after all along?" she said finally once her heaving sobs of shame subsided. He didn't answer and continued to maintain the silence the taxi journey home.

It had become beautifully crystalised to her in that moment, when she watched Mark and Darren facing off. She had no defence for him. She didn't want to. She saw him how Darren saw him. A lecherous, abusive prick. Mark had asked her what had changed. He had changed. She had changed. Everything had changed. He was once her weighted blanket of security, holding her down to earth, keeping her present and focused. It felt more like the blanket was smothering her now, making her too warm and dizzy and unable to think. She tried to imagine the perspective from someone from the outside like Jen, like Darren. Why were they together? Was she using him for money? Was he using her for sex? It had never felt this way for Teeny but as the dust had settled in her chaotic mind, she found it hard to focus on why they were still together. She should have left after the first slap, the first punch, the first kick. She realised it went much further though, the red flags that were all there. The questioning, the checking her phone constantly, tracking her phone, the shouting. All perhaps small things that had gradually taken away small and large fragments of her already fragile mind and soul. She had been believing for a long time that she deserved this poor treatment, a fitting punishment for being unfaithful. She could not have her cake and eat it. She could not have an affair with Prince Charming and get to marry him too.

"Do you want one?" Mark asked quietly as he poured himself a drink when they arrived home.

"No, I want to leave," she responded, the words were out of her mouth before she had time to process the answer in her head. She wanted to listen to her gut so she didn't add anything, just stood and waited for the shattering of glass. He didn't respond but raised his eyebrows once in surprise and took a long drink of his whisky.

"That bad, am I?" he said finally and broke off into tears facing away from her. He was easier to hate when he was angry, when his teeth were gritted, his words were loud and his hands were rough. Teeny took a long breath and released it slowly and quietly to keep her thoughts clear. The guilt of tearing the plaster off tugged at her heart and hurt her throat when she tried to speak.

"Yes. You are," she answered sounding sure of herself but not feeling as confident as her voice suggested. She backed out of the room and walked into the spare room unsure of what to do next but couldn't stand to look at his hurt face any longer. She wished she had waited until the morning, until he was sober, until he was away to work. She'd have been able to pack her things and sneak them out but realised this was a very familiar pattern. *'You're a fucking coward'*. Ryan's truthful words ringing in her ears. She started opening drawers and opening bags, wary that he was listening to her and had already poured another drink.

"Where will you go then?" he asked softly and sincerely as he cradled his glass in the doorway.

Teeny didn't have an answer. She had done the research when she knew she was leaving Ryan, before she decided to live with Mark. She knew some rough options of who to contact to present herself as homeless and how to go about it. She didn't want to return home or anywhere near it to face the humiliation she would surely receive. She had made her bed and should be lying in it. She shrugged and bit her lip trying to keep her tears concealed as she packed her bags.

"I don't want you to leave, please stay," he continued.

"You don't want to trust me either though, Mark. You don't want to believe that I only wanted you, love you and am not just some daft wee tart fucking anyone and everyone," she broke off letting her tears fall freely down her face. "Did you really believe I was shagging Darren, shagging Michael, shagging any creep that glanced at me sideways when your back was turned?" He looked to the floor and shook his head so she continued, "Then why treat me like this? You've physically hurt me in more ways than I've accepted from anyone and worse, you've made me frightened of you, worried about coming home to you. Well, I'm not frightened anymore. I don't know what the fuck I'm going to do but I am *done* doing this. I really, really think you should get help. I want that for you," she said as she finished zipping up her clumsily packed bags.

As she stood up, he blocked the doorway and looked into her eyes for a long time, thinking of his next move but stood aside to let her cross into the master bedroom to take some items from there. He moved to the foot of the bed rubbing his mouth and chin with his hand either trying to pluck words out or muffling what he really wanted to say.

"You're making a mistake, Colette. Don't do this. I'll go and speak to Darren, sort it out. I'll tell him I was drunk and that's never happened before. I'll make it right so you can still work there. I won't give you shit anymore, please sweetheart.

I'll make it right; I'll get the help. I love you," he said sitting on the edge of the bed looking up at her with earnest, pleading eyes.

'I'll pretend it didn't happen' was what Teeny heard. It would have been easy to walk over, to hold him and let all his easy words soak into her skin. To feel like home again when she was in his arms, breathing him in. She couldn't.

"I need to go, Mark. This isn't what I want. I love you too but you are breaking me," she tried to talk through choked, strangled tears, "please get help. Please don't follow me. If you make this difficult for me, I'll go to the police and Darren will be my witness. Just let me go, OK?"

His eyes squinted in anger at her use of Darren's name as her ally. She knew she had control here, in this small window, and she needed to use it before her anxious mind got the better of her and her resolve crumbed.

"You better fuck off then; Darren will be waiting." His soft tone evaporating as he stood, sank his drink and carelessly tossed the glass on top of the drawers, letting it fall and roll on its side. He marched out of the room and into the lounge, slamming the door behind him. She hurriedly grabbed her bags, pulling them into the stairwell, trying to grab them all at once so she didn't need to go back inside. When she pulled the front door to close it, she listened in, waiting for banging, shouting, chaos, it never came.

She asked the taxi driver to hold on for five to ten minutes while she jumped out. She walked along the street of brightly decorated houses and waited for Darren to come out of his mother's bungalow. She took a seat on the low wall lining the driveway when she saw the hall light come on. It was a clear night and the stars were glittering over the sky.

"Why did you no' just come ti the door, it's fuckin' freezing oot here, Teen," Darren said as he sat down lighting his cigarette.

"I'm not staying. I just wanted to see you quickly before…" she broke herself off not quite sure what she wanted to say.

"Are you alright, pal? That was a fuckin' madness in there the night. I got the fright of my life when I saw you like that, could've killed that slimey wee cunt," he said, then slowly exhaled his smoke.

"I'm alright and thank you. Look, I asked to see you 'cause I need to give you your keys, for the pub like. I'm leaving. I have to get away from here," Teeny said.

Darren wanted to laugh, to mock her and make a quip about her 'going to find herself' and how she sounded like something from a shite film. He knew better though. He'd watched Teeny grow up under the wings of people who never seemed to love her properly. She stood a chance if she actually fucked off.

"Where the fuck are you gonna go, it's nearly fuckin Christmas?" he said slightly panicked for her clicking on that she was making this up as she went along.

She shrugged again, like when Mark had asked her, only this time she smiled. She wasn't afraid, she knew she would figure it out. She knew now what she didn't want and couldn't have so would walk in the opposite direction of that.

"Ach, I'll be fine. Even if I end up working in a bar in Benidorm, at least it'll be sunny and miles away from here, eh?" she joked, elbowing him.

"And him?" Darren asked, his face darkening.

"Gone. Done," she said with sincere finality but her chest ached heavy and cold knowing she meant it.

He slowly nodded. "Dinnae be a stranger though, eh? There'll always be a shift for you or a seat at the bar." He smiled as he took Teeny's lead as she stood to walk back towards her waiting taxi.

"Thanks, Darren. Now fuck off back inside, your pizza will be freezing!" She tried to laugh. To avoid showing her his teary eyes, he pulled her in for a hug, the first time they'd ever been this close so it felt tense and awkward at first but she rested her head against his chest and listened to his wheezing for a minute and smelled his aftershave mixed with smoke.

"Look after yourself, Colette. Really," he said as he released her.

His use of her name made her smile rather than make her jump to attention. She walked back to the taxi and gave the address to the nearest Premier Inn. She didn't want a halfway house at her parents' again, she wanted a fresh start and space to figure out what that meant without needing to explain herself to them. She checked her phone, he hadn't called. Maybe he would assume that she would just return to her parents and he could collect her like a parcel from the post office after 'she'd calmed down'. Once she'd checked in and dumped her bags on the floor, she sat in the middle of the double bed and put her phone on charge. She deleted her entire call log and all text messages. She took a long breath in and let her thumb hover over the phone, 'block number'. She clicked it then locked her phone. She could feel her anxiety catching up to the knee jerk decisions she'd been making since Darren's pizza hit the floor in the pub. She could feel her breath become shallower and her hands become sweaty.

"The lamp, the bed, my bag, my phone, the TV. The traffic, doors slamming, the heating, someone walking in the corridor. The bed, my phone, my jacket. Cigarette smoke, hand wash. The biscuit from the tea and coffee tray."

Teeny felt her chest move up and down more gradually as she repeated the technique she'd been practicing on Jen's advice; name aloud five things you see, four things you hear, three things you can touch, two things you can smell, one thing you can taste. She kicked off her boots and stripped down to her t-shirt and underwear and let the tightly fitted duvet snug tightly around her as she let the QVC channel in the room be her lullaby to sleep.

13. 19 March 2019

Teeny sat up and watched the waves sneak closer to her feet before drifting backwards again. She'd been listening to a new podcast on Jen's recommendation even though she found Russell Brand's voice a little irritating. She took out her earphones and consciously listened to the waves, their rough crashing easing into a slow fizzy pour as they got closer to her. It was barely past breakfast time and here she was sitting in the sand watching the tide coming in. It gave her enormous peace when she sat out like this in the morning and it helped her stay exactly where she was, where she needed to be to get through the day and stay focused.

"Is it aye, it's still raining? Well, that's it, March goes out like a lion and in like a lamb, eh?" Teeny asked as she kept her promise to herself and contacted her mother for her usual monthly phone call just to check in.

"And do you not see Mark at all anymore then, is that aw finished aye?" her mother asked with disappointment stinging her voice.

"Aye, Mum, all finished. Just me out here. Listen, I'll be back home in a couple of weeks. I'll pop in and see you then OK, I'll need to head for my shift. Love you, tell Dad I said hiya," Teeny finished as she mentally checked off her 'to-do' list.

She breathed in the morning air and pulled little piles of sand together not quite ready to get up. She checked her phone and emailed Jen back to let her know her thoughts on the recent podcast episode. Curiosity had often tugged her conscious when writing to Jen, she wanted to know how her upstairs neighbour was doing; was he OK? Was he alone? When she first got her new phone, she was by herself, in an airport for the first time in her life. She was afraid and excited and overwhelmed. She watched as parents entertained their children, commuters typed on laptops and lovers snuggled into each other to rest. She wanted to call him. To hear his voice. The toxic weight on her shoulders almost letting her phone him since she knew his number by heart. She knew it would defeat the whole purpose of every step she'd taken so far. He no longer had access to her, he couldn't find her, unless she wanted him to. Teeny found Jen easily enough from her local yoga class website info and sent her an email to let her know she wouldn't be around anymore. From there, they kept in contact almost every week sending various links to music, podcasts or articles to read or Teeny sending the odd smug beach picture. Neither one of the women had mentioned 'Mr Daddy Issues' upstairs and she was grateful for it but it meant she would have to rely on her own self-control to fully cut out the poisoned parts of her.

As she stood up, she brushed the sand off her jeans and lifted her boots to make her way back to the hotel. She pulled on her apron and said good morning to Nettie, simultaneously sticking the kettle on to warm them both up. The sun was strong today but it was bitterly cold outside. The sea air, always beautiful and biting. Teeny had found herself at home in the small hotel. It was more like a bed and breakfast but a large, grand hotel would not have been suitable on Barra so most of the accommodation on the island seemed to have a 'granny's house' feel about it. Tourism was slow at this time of year but Teeny made herself indispensable to Nettie and Wullie, the elderly couple who had no family and were struggling with some of the workload. Teeny helped them redecorate the dining area and bar and helped them develop a website to drum up some more business as the visiting season began in a few weeks.

She had originally come to stay for a weekend with the intention of hopping on to some of the other islands but her savings had run their course in just under two months and she wasn't ready to return to any kind of normality or routine yet. They had allowed her to stay on and rather than pay a wage, she was paid with somewhere warm and safe to sleep. Some days, she would only see three other people, including Nettie and Wullie and other days, perhaps a handful with their dogs at a distance on the beach. It was a dramatic difference from the scenes in London, where she had flown to in her haste just a couple of days before Christmas last year.

Teeny woke up that morning in December in the Premier Inn after her rash getaway, groggy and hungover despite her sobriety the night before. She skimmed her hand over the perfectly tucked side of the bed, untouched as she lay on only one side. She picked up her phone, four missed calls from this morning. All from a Glasgow based landline number. Mark's work number, she assumed. The strange numbers on her screen made her feel sick. The bed was warm and the room was quiet but she felt panicked. She wanted to go home to feel safe, to at least know what would happen next.

Sitting up, she cradled her legs and squeezed her hands together tightly. She switched on the TV to hear some familiarity in the presenters talking about Christmas shopping or what to watch, it comforted her. Teeny nibbled on one of the complimentary custard cremes and watched the competition information slide and pop over the screen. An all-expenses paid trip to London for New Year's including theatre tickets. She watched the happy shopper's bustle in the busy streets, the smiling faces, the anonymity of them all. Teeny opened her online banking app, she'd had a decent bit saved between her half of the deposit money she didn't end up needing and some money she had been saving to buy Mark a watch for his Christmas. She booked a flight for the next day, found a reasonable hotel and decided that was what she needed. A completely different place to start again, somewhere she could never be found. The novelty of the big smoke had lasted around six days and after that Teeny spent most of her time either in the Tesco two doors down from her hotel or sat at the window eating Dairylea dunkers and drinking gin and lemonade from a mug, terrified to leave the room. The city was too loud, too chaotic. Even if she wasn't moving around or doing much herself, it seemed the people and the buildings were always vibrating, never winding down and she was failing to keep pace. Her panic attacks had returned and were becoming more frequent. She knew it didn't help that she wasn't sleeping properly, wasn't eating properly and spent most of her waking hours either slightly drunk or hungover. She decided to return home just before Valentine's Day, to Scotland at least. She booked her train to

Oban and decided to call the pub to talk to Darren, her anxiety telling her Mark would be waiting at the train station, somehow knowing she was back over the border.

"It's good to hear from ye, wee yin," Darren shouted down the phone sounding genuinely relieved. "Where eh ye?"

"London, for now anyway. I'm heading back up the road soon but just wanted to check in, see how folk are?" Teeny had tried to test the waters as subtly as possible.

"He's no' been near, Teen. 'Hink he kens the score if he tried coming in here."

Teeny blushed but was grateful she didn't need to explain herself further to Darren, that he'd been able to pick up on her troubled thoughts.

"Yer da keeps asking for ye though. Unless you were gee'in him half-priced pints, I'd say he's missin ye," he continued and laughed to himself. Guilt stung her throat a little. She hadn't called her parents to explain she was leaving. She didn't think it would matter since she didn't live with them and couldn't be sure they wouldn't have told Mark where she ended up if he did decide to turn up there to collect his wayward, skittish girlfriend. Teeny reassured him she would pop in soon and made her way closer to home and promised him she would contact her mother to let her know she was OK.

She'd been staying with Nettie and Wullie for six weeks or so since she arrived on the island. It had been the calm, idyllic atmosphere she'd craved from her hotel window in London but she still felt something was missing. Homesick would have been the wrong word to use. There was nothing and no one to go back to. Not really. She hadn't seen Mark for three months and his lack of interest in social media meant she couldn't even scroll to find a picture of him. She knew that this was a blessing but she swallowed the renewed realisation like grit each time he popped into her head. 'I miss him', 'I still love him', 'I'm lonely'.

"We havin' tea or we havin' tar, hen?" Nettie laughed breaking Teeny's distant thoughts. "You're miles away, pet. Here, let me, away and bring in that delivery, will ye?" She tutted but continued to laugh while she took over making the tea as Teeny's brain caught up with her feet that had started to walk towards the door.

Once she'd returned with the boxes, she gratefully lifted her cup and cradled it to warm her hands. "You can always come back once you've visited home, you know. Work the season, it's like night and day here – people from aw oor come, it's heaving!" Nettie offered as if trying to answer a conversation Teeny was having internally.

"Thanks, Nettie. That's really kind. You and Wullie have been amazing but I'll need to get doon the road and sort myself out." She half smiled and rubbed her kind boss cum landlord's arm as she went back to the boxes to unpack them.

She had never explained much of her background or reason for travelling alone to them but they seemed to just telepathically sense that she was troubled, running maybe. They never quizzed or questioned her or pressed her for more details when she let out small accidental slips of information about her journey to date. They just seemed glad of the new company and her knack for numbers and websites. An arrangement that suited all three of them.

The logical part of Teeny's brain knew that Mark wasn't going to arrive on the beach by plane or appear at Nettie's door on a rainy night to convince her he was changed and that she should come home with him. It didn't stop her feeling like she was running though. Always looking over her shoulder waiting on someone or even if it was just her own thoughts sneaking up on her. She felt she owed herself some proper closure in her life so she could move on fully and realised that beginning again or having 'a fresh start' was more about her mindset than a location. She couldn't keep running forever. On 3 April, she took her final walk along the cold white sand in her bare feet and promised herself that she would return to this stunning island, not because she was running away from where she was, but because she was coming towards a place of beauty, peace and calm.

The weather on her journey back to Falkirk had been atrocious. The rain was relentless and the wind whipped at her face and hair and pushed her around until she managed to navigate her way into the train station. When she arrived at her parents, she was surprised to see her mother fully dressed and her father home before dinnertime awaiting her arrival. They greeted her warmly enough and they busied themselves talking about London and Barra and how Alec and Denise were meant to go to Skye for their honeymoon but never made it because Teeny got the chickenpox.

"And did ye hear Stuart Matheson died?" Alec said, not quite sadly but with a very serious look on his face that Teeny didn't usually see when he was recalling all the names from the Falkirk Herald obits.

"Who the fuck is Stuart Math…" *Stuarty, coffin dodgers*, Teeny realised mid-sentence. "Well, one down, I suppose, eh," Teeny said coldly without lifting her eyes away from the glass of water she was drinking.

"Teeny, for fuck sake. Don't talk like that. He was a good friend of your dad's!" Denise shook her head as she admonished her daughter but Alec simply looked at the table and nervously scratched at the back of his hand.

"Sorry, Dad, when's the funeral?" Teeny said with the same cold tone.

"Eh, Friday, pal. It's Friday," he answered quietly.

She nodded quickly and nervously, trying to suppress the intense nausea that had clouded over her.

"OK, I'll come along with you two then. Pay my respects," Teeny offered.

Denise seemed appeased enough that her daughter had corrected her rude behaviour but Alec didn't really respond at all, other than stand to go to the fridge for another can then shuffle off into the living room.

It was still raining on the Friday morning when they all crowded into the Crematorium for Stuarty's service. Unfamiliar family members looking soggy, sad and cold, hovered in the front row and the rest of the pews were a scattering of Cross Keys regulars and some from the bowling club. Teeny scanned the room looking for tears or relieved relatives, tuning out the minister's journey through 'our brother' Stuart's life and the haunting melody of the Old Rugged Cross. They made their way back to the pub in the rain and Lynne had spread out pots of soup and trays of sandwiches covered in flimsy cling film. Teeny, almost instinctively, helped unwrap the sandwiches and hand out bowls. Anything to keep busy, avoid conversation. She found Darren in the kitchen looking for napkins.

"Top shelf, dafty," she teased and he pulled her into a bear like grip.

The day sat strangely with them all. Not necessarily a loveable character to be mourned and missed but a piece of their existence gone nonetheless.

"You hingin' around for a while then?" Darren asked while handing her the napkins.

"No sure yet, to be honest. Just felt like it was the right time to come home and sort some shit out, ken?" She guessed, taking the pile from him. He didn't know, but he nodded anyway. Teeny was surprised that her mother had stayed out this long. She had been drinking wine and talking to people she probably hadn't seen in at least two years. She had sat with Louis and Sandra, Deek and his wife and looked relaxed, comfortable. Even though it had never been acknowledged aloud, Louis would never look at her the same way again after how she treated 'that nice laddie' Ryan by sleeping with Mark behind his back. Even worse, she didn't want to entangle herself in small talk with Deek in case either one mentioned his usual 'acquaintance from the pub'. She decided it best to hang around the bar near her dad and Darren. As the hours ticked on, Teeny could feel the waves of alcohol pool and swish over her, washing her with courage and she found herself talking to the regulars from the other side of the bar. She hadn't been really drunk, like this, for a couple of months, since drinking alone in her bleak hotel room in London. It took over her quickly and she stumbled around attempting to help clear up paper plates and glasses.

"Leave it, Teen, you're no workin'," Darren would remind her while taking glasses away from her before she broke them. Stuarty's family had cleared out pretty quickly so by teatime there was only a handful of 'mourners' left. Rab had sat accepting drinks most of the afternoon, feeling the empty space at the table beside him where his fallen comrade should be.

"It'll be weird just him sitting there now, eh?" Lynne had whispered as she passed the bar to hand in more glasses.

"Hopefully he'll be put out his misery soon too," Teeny had said louder than she intended but the more she drank, the worse her guts churned as she found herself staring into the corner.

She'd felt a cold rage slam against her with the news of Stuarty's death as if something within her died too, without warning. She felt cheated, as if the poisonous shame and troubled memories that crept into her mind would now stay like that forever; poisonous and troubled. She had never imagined herself having a conversation with either of these men to confront them for fear that her mind had misinterpreted something or created a memory that was false. She couldn't bear the humiliation if she was wrong. Now she would never have the chance even if she wanted to. Or perhaps, only half a chance. Her anger and fear and disgust had slowly been building and now as she sat and stared at Rab while sipping her drink with heavy, drunk eyes she wanted to throw the glass at him. She wanted to tip the table upwards or yank him by his limp, sparse hair and slam his face onto the table. Teeny bit her lip hard to suppress the urge, her hands shook and she almost knocked over her drink as she turned to pick it up to sip at it, sucking at the ice since the glass was empty. Darren and Lynne looked at each other awkwardly and Darren gave Lynne a warning shake of the head as if to signal not to challenge Teeny's outburst.

"Another, hen?" Alec offered from behind her.

"Aye. A double please," she responded without turning to face him, or thank him.

Her father accepted his change and walked around to the barstool on the other side of Teeny so he could position himself in between her and Rab, making her see him.

"I think I owe you an apology, wee yin," Alec started.

The sincere look on his face caught Teeny off guard and he had her full attention.

Her mouth went dry. "For what?" she asked.

"For no sayin' anything to that cunt. What he did ti ye." He shook his head and took a long mouthful of his pint.

Teeny could feel sweat beads rolling down her back and her face flush hard. Of all the places and times they could have had this conversation, he was choosing here and now.

"I wish ye wid have said somethin' hen, I'd have fuckin' killed him. Treatin' ma Teeny like that. Acting like butter widni fuckin melt in his mooth."

Teeny could feel her jaw tighten and tears wet her mascara.

"You knew?" she barely whispered.

Alec nodded as he gulped at his drink again. "Well, no' at first. I didni' want to pry when I saw the bruises but Darren had telt me what happened and that's why ye disappeared. Dinnae worry though, yer maw disnae know."

Mark, she realised. He was talking about Mark, not Stuarty, not Rab.

"Didn't want to pry?" She laughed darkly and took a long drink. "Ye dinnae like getting involved, dae ye, Dad? Dinnae want to make a scene?" she added dramatically.

Denise had clocked the tense conversation and her whole table was now watching them. "Well, he was your fuckin' fella, hen, and—"

"And you're MA FUCKIN DAD!" Teeny shouted, interrupting him and stared at him wide-eyed.

"Haw, cool it wee yin, it's a wake, mind," Darren gently reminded her from behind the bar. Teeny caught her bearings and stepped off the barstool.

"Don't worry about it, Dad, I'm used to it wi' you. Wouldn't want you 'prying' and accidentally saving me," she said acidly using elaborate air quotes.

"The fuck eh you on about?" Alec asked, bemused.

"Him," she answered coldly pointing at Rab, "and him," she added while pointing up the way before correcting herself and pointing downwards.

Rab, who had been watching the two of them told Alec to take Teeny up the road if she couldn't handle her drink.

"Aw fuck up, you dirty auld bastard!" Teeny roared across the pub and brought her accusing finger back towards her father's face and seethed more quietly between her teeth

"I-I was a fuckin. Bairn. And your wee pals. Your mates…" She trailed off as realisation rolled over Alec, knocking him back against the bar. "Aye. I thought so." She continued, "And where were you? Right. Fucking. Here." She punctuated each word with a sharp jabbing finger into his chest, tears rolling down her face and burning her throat as she spoke.

She couldn't control it any longer, the bile that she had been holding down anytime they had looked at her or spoke to her. She was free, she'd said it, wrong or not.

"Naw, hen. Naw. You've made a mistake," Alec tried to protest quietly but his own shame as the useless drunk father was seeping in, throwing the images back up at him like a slide projector whether he was ready for the next picture or not. He'd wanted it to have been his imagination too. Surely, she wouldn't still have worked here and had to speak to them if that had been happening? He'd allowed himself to believe that the drink had played tricks with his eyes. She was a happy wee girl. She loved picking the horses.

"Teeny, away up the road ti yer bed. This is Stuarty's day. You'll no ruin it wi yer fuckin nonsense." Rab had stood up to scold her, unaware of the exact exchange of words between Teeny and Alec.

"Ma fuckin' nonsense?" Teeny screamed back.

There was an uproar of voices and activity as Rab and the cronies at his table stood to defend themselves and Alec trying to frantically hold Teeny back who was now trying to screech and scream her way towards him.

Darren had appeared on her side flanked by Alec and Denise who were pulling her back in towards the kitchen while she screamed and kicked. The wounded animal. Darren pulled the kitchen door shut leaving the four of them inside as Teeny thrashed into the cooker throwing plates and cups and anything she could reach to the floor. She had never experienced such blood curdling rage and didn't want to let up despite the cries of her mother and roars of her father. Darren took her face and held her begging her to stop, to calm down. She whimpered and slowed under his grasp and sobbed heavily into his chest, feeling the intensity of her rage dissipate to be replaced with humiliation, guilt, fear and pain.

When she'd come to her senses, she stood and took in the scenes of her destruction in the tiny kitchen.

"I should never have come back here," Teeny cried softly to herself.

Alec hovered a hand near her shoulder and hesitated whether to put it there to comfort her but let it fall back by his side.

"You'll go out there and apologise. Now. That was a bloody disgrace, Teeny," Denise said sternly, finding her voice after getting over the shock of what she had just witnessed.

Teeny and Alec looked at each other, Alec bit his lip and looked to the floor.

"I love you, Mum, and I'm sorry if I embarrassed you, but I'll do no such fucking thing," she said containing the renewed anger she could feel burning through her finger tips.

Denise looked at her incredulously and scoffed at her then walked back through to the bar to collect her bag and leave or so Teeny assumed.

"Sorry about the plates, Darren," Teeny offered as she shook out of his hold and tried to pick up the pieces on the floor.

"Leave it, wee yin, honestly, it's fine. I'll get it later. I'll leave you two to it," he added awkwardly as he shuffled around Alec and went back out to serve and try to restore some harmony in the madness.

"I should never have come back," she said more quietly and shook her head.

"No. You shouldni huv," Alec agreed, letting his own eyes tear up.

Teeny let her mouth open in shock, ready to tear into Alec and let him have the fury she had been robbed of through in the bar. "I really made a cunt of it, Teenytote," he sniffed.

The use of the pet name only he used for her as a child made her stomach flip and her anger melt into sorrow.

"You should stay as far away from this shitehole as possible. Maybe get some help, like your mum?" he added genuinely.

Teeny realised this was as close as she would get. She wouldn't get a formal apology and true ownership of his abuse of alcohol masking his ability to see what was happening to his child a few feet away. He wouldn't be able to look her in the eye and admit what his adult eyes probably saw through blurred vision, which could fill the gaps in her disturbing dreams. He would tell her to run away, to get help because she was the one with 'the problem'. That way, he wouldn't need to choke on his own guilt anytime he had to look into his daughter's eyes. She bit back her response and changed it to a simple goodbye, a half-hearted instruction to him to go up the road and make sure her mum was OK. She tapped her pockets in her dress to make sure her phone and purse were still there and took a left at the kitchen door to leave via the lounge. She didn't trust herself on that side of the bar anymore.

She marched along the pavement, unsure of where she was going and kicking herself for leaving her jacket. At least the rain had stopped. When the pub was out of sight, she slowed her pace, aware of the headlights that had been lighting her direction for the last couple of minutes and never passing her. Normally, she would be poised with her keys between her fingers or her phone in hand but she didn't feel in immediate danger. She already knew it was his car before she turned around to stop and look.

"What are you doing here?" Teeny tried to keep her voice controlled as she spoke to Mark through the driver's window he'd rolled down. The first time she had seen him in three months.

"Could ask you the same thing, I thought you had disappeared off the face of the Earth?" he responded coolly.

"What. Are you doing here, Mark?" She deliberately enunciated each word to try to stop her voice from pitching.

"Deek. He texted me," he stopped himself explaining further.

Teeny wondered if Deek knew why they were no longer together, had he sent a text to let him know she'd resurfaced, ready to be hunted? Or that she was currently screeching the place down in the local pub decrying the dead and calling his mourning friend a beast. She glanced around nervously seeing if anyone was walking by. The roads were dead. She bit her lip to suppress the tears of humiliation she could feel building as she remembered who would have all seen her act out in such a dramatic, ridiculous way.

"I can go. I-I just wanted to make sure you were OK. He said you were quite upset," he said softly.

"I'm pretty fucking far from OK," she quoted, from his favourite film and smiled slightly to shift the mood from feeling so vulnerable.

14. 6 April 2019

He slept so soundly. Teeny wondered if this was how people who regularly had one-night stands felt in the morning. Do they wait until their soul mate from the night before wakes up? Or do they just grab their clothes and tiptoe out to avoid any awkward conversations or goodbyes? She'd already mentally clocked where her dress had slid to the floor and where her bra had landed after it had been tossed but she had no idea where her phone or purse were so there was no subtly sneaking out, she'd make too much noise. This was no stranger that would be grateful she slipped out the door before he woke up. The last time she was in this bedroom, she was hurriedly scraping together her belongings to escape his oppression and jealousy. She rubbed her face and tried to retrace her steps from the night before. How had she managed to end up in Mark's bed just days after returning home. She scolded herself for being so weak.

"Can I take you somewhere, up the road to your mum's maybe?" Mark had offered.

Teeny really didn't want to see her mother. Denise didn't know any better and to her, Teeny looked like a drunken, dramatic pollution who had embarrassed her in front of her friends and neighbours. She'd probably never come back out to socialise now. The thought flooded Teeny's face with new guilt. She didn't want to have to explain all of this to her. Not tonight. So, she shook her head but couldn't think of where else she could go to decompress from the chaos she'd just set free.

"Do you fancy a drive then, just to get out of the cold?" he continued to offer but Teeny who had been shaking her head gently started to shake more emphatically, her subconscious reminding her to keep clear.

"No funny business, I promise." He half laughed, signalling his scouts honour.

Teeny let out a deep sigh. His smile softened her resolve and she was freezing.

"No funny business," she repeated with a warning finger as she walked around and slid into the passenger side.

Her senses were overcome with the familiarity of it; the shape of his hand on the gearstick, the sound of his music playing far too low, the feeling of the seat under her palms, the smell of his polo mints. The memories lurched in her stomach and she could feel the acid of the alcohol climbing her throat, she swallowed in distaste.

"You alright? There's a bottle of water in your side bit." He offered as he pulled back out onto the road. "It's still sealed, Colette," he added sardonically, catching Teeny's face as she looked at the bottle of water.

They drove around for a long time in silence and Teeny felt pangs of homesickness looking at the beautiful buildings and streets she had missed. Mark eventually parked up and let the music continue to play, filling the gaps between her taking tiny mouthfuls of water. She watched the colours change intermittently on the magnificent Kelpies in the distance.

She'd hated all the hype when they were being built and never believed for a minute they would bring scores of tourists to Falkirk just to see 'metal horsey heeds' as they were described in the pub. They were truly something to behold though, especially at night.

"I've really missed you," he said quietly as he turned to face her.

"I missed you too," she responded honestly but focused on the lights while they changed to blue.

"You look…well?" he attempted but Teeny raised her eyebrows at him questioning his definition of 'well' since her face was puffy and red and stained with mascara and her curled hair from this morning was now a mass of tufts and cow licks from all the wrestling to try and contain her rage earlier. "Apart from the hair maybe." He laughed and instinctively put his hand out to tuck a curl behind her ear, making Teeny flinch.

"Fuck, sorry. Just a habit," he apologised and put both hands back on the wheel as if to handcuff himself to avoid touching her involuntarily. "Where did you go?" he asked after a long pause.

Teeny thought about her answer, the secret was out anyway, she was back so she figured it was redundant holding back any information now. She told him about London and how it had been too busy for her and how she ended up spending most of her time (and money) on gin.

"Gin? Since when do you drink gin?" he asked, amused.

"I don't. I drank it with lemonade to kill the taste a bit. It just, reminded me of you, I guess. I know. It's really sad." She laughed at herself a little and cringed at her oversharing but he didn't laugh.

He managed to hide his disdain for her using lemonade but looked at her wistfully and as she turned to look at him, she thought she might start crying again.

Instead, she babbled on about her polarised move to Barra and all its wonders and character. The feel of the cold, white sand under her feet and the sound of the water coming in. How sweet Nettie and Wullie were and their adorable boutique hotel and how she had help do it up with them. She told him how she hoped it was getting busy and the improved website and booking system were working well.

"It sounds really lovely, what made you come back then?" he asked sincerely not taking his eyes away from hers.

Teeny could feel the new hot tears fall down her face, she squeezed her fingertips together to concentrate on the sensation.

"I'm not sure. Unfinished business I thought but I just seem to be making an arse of myself so fuck knows," she answered and roughly rubbed the tears away.

"You fancy a wee drink, I'm not sure I've got any lemonade in, mind you?" he teased.

She nodded slowly, letting her body answer for her. Her body wanted to dull out the tense grip on the back of her neck, the tides in her stomach and the heavy ache in her chest. She wanted to drink and it was well after 10 pm now so she'd have no joy in any shops and didn't want to be alone. Her unconscious mind seemed to be slipping, the 'keep clear' sign blunting. It, like her, also wanted this a little longer, his smile, his voice, his kind words.

She looked away from her reflection in the large mirror in the hallway as she untied her boots. She followed him through to the breakfast bar and breathed in the familiar air while she stroked along the bar and took her usual seat on one of the stools. It was so strange, the foreign views of a room she'd been in many times before, similar to a return from a holiday. Everything appears to have moved a couple of centimetres to the left, or so it would seem.

He poured them both a gin and tonic, adding extra tonic for Teeny. She sipped at it trying not to let her face screw up too obviously.

"So, what about you? How have you been, what have you been up to? I've just been chatting shite about myself this whole time?" she asked hurriedly.

She became aware that he was the main reason she had disappeared for as long as she did and now, the minute it had turned to shit, he was right there to scoop her up, rescue her. It felt strange, awkward. She felt on display like a tiny, helpless bird in a shattered glass box.

He took a sip and licked his lips. "Oh, the usual, trying to mend a broken heart, working, trying to come to terms with how badly I fucked it up, going to the gym. You know, the usual?" He smiled sadly and they both laughed a little awkwardly.

"Fuck, this is weird, isn't it? I should go. I'm just…" She stood up flapping slightly.

"No. Honestly, Colette. I'm fine. I get it. I really just wanted to make sure you were alright knowing it was that creep's funeral. And when Deek contacted me, I couldn't resist seeing you again. I love you. I just wanted to look out for you," he explained as he walked slowly towards her putting his hands on her shoulders.

She hung her head and started to whimper, feeling like a child. He took her in closer to his chest, rubbing her back and soothing her.

"Sshh, don't cry, sweetheart. Here, why don't you get some sleep?" He signalled to the bedroom and continued, answering the panicked expression on her face, "I'll take the couch, you should get some rest, you're all over the place. Scout's honour, mind." He smiled and she nodded in agreement.

She knew exhaustion was creeping in and her emotions had done full circuits all day long. She'd seen too many ghosts today. She needed to sleep.

She walked into the bedroom and looked at the perfectly made bed. She crawled over it to where she used to sleep and pulled the throw over her, fully clothed, too tired to undress. She pulled his pillow closer to her and drank in his smell, letting her lips sweep over the material. She moved the pillow between her thighs and squeezed, squirming her legs and trying to get comfortable. She felt restless and uneasy not being able to see him but knowing he was in the same space as her. It was unnerving.

Her higher self knew she should have walked away from his car, never entertained him, let alone come back into the lion's den and make herself at home in his bed. Teeny realised she'd left her higher self on the barstool in the Cross Keys, possibly on the isle of Barra. Her loneliness and regretful thoughts and dark headspace had led her here. Despite her racing mind and her tight chest, she felt a tingling in her gut and a weakness in her knees that she hadn't in such a long time whenever he looked at her for too long and when he put his hands on her arms. She pulled her weight around in the

182

bed again trying to switch off but she couldn't. Teeny sat up and swung her legs onto the carpet to look out of the window. As she walked back through to the lounge, he was sat at the bay window, reading his phone.

He looked over the screen and poorly tried to conceal his surprise. "Can't sleep?" he asked slyly.

She shook her head once and hovered at the breakfast bar before walking over to remove the phone from his hand and kissed him softly on the lips. He was enjoying this, her making the moves. He didn't kiss her back at first until she softly licked the underneath of his top lip then sat herself in his lap, straddling him.

"What is this?" he asked quietly as he pushed back the hair from her face. She shrugged softly not really sure herself. She already knew it was a bad idea, a seed that was planted when she first felt his headlights on her on the road. Nothing she was doing seemed to make sense anymore. If she felt anger, she said it. If she felt rage, she threw it. Teeny was lost and scrambling for any scrap of good feeling or normality she could find.

When she lay in the morning light, watching him sleep, she knew this was it. She'd felt empty and his weight on her felt heavy and awkward. She willed him to finish quickly. This wasn't love. Not anymore. She felt guilty knowing she had changed the boundaries of their fragile conversation, not him. She shifted onto her side hoping she could slide out and at least have her dress back on to have this conversation. Mark roused slightly and pulled her in, nuzzling her back with his nose and chin.

"Well, this was unexpected," he spoke in whispers into her skin.

"Was it?" She half laughed. "You mean you didn't see us here when you picked me up, when you got in your car to come find me, when you received that text?" she added more icily than she intended.

He traced a finger down her shoulder over her waist and hips. "I just wanted to make sure you were OK, you were the one who kissed me, remember?"

Teeny felt herself become terse but knew he was right. Despite what his intentions might have been, she was the one to climb out of the bed and onto his lap.

"I know, I'm sorry," she reflected quietly. "It shouldn't have happened though. This," she added, shaking her head.

She climbed out of the bed and tiptoed into the hall quickly to pick up her bra and dress, blushing at the thought of being seen so naked in the cold light of day. It seemed absurd since he had seen her skin so many times before and last night, he had held her and provided a comfort she thought she was missing. That had disappeared with the night, he felt like a stranger now and she wanted to be somewhere else, she wanted to feel clean. As she picked up her phone and purse from the breakfast bar, she slowly walked back into the bedroom to Mark who was now sitting up, looking puzzled.

"Colette, you don't have to run off. Stay, have a coffee. Let's just talk?" he proposed.

"What's there to talk about Mark? Honestly? I mean, last night was nice but that's all it was. We're not getting back together, nothing has changed. For me, anyway," she responded firmly.

She had felt strong and assertive, now that she was dressed. The words she'd practised if she ever saw him again during her lonely hours on the beach. Reality began to set in as she looked at him, waiting for his response, that she was standing where he had choked her after the Christmas party, shoved her on another occasion and gripped her by the collar while screaming into her face on another. The memories looped through her mind and sent her heart racing and her hands trembling. She sidestepped into the hall to grab her boots but brought them into the room to put them on so she could see where he was, could see him coming if he was to get up to attack her. He looked at her pensively for a long time then threw back the cover leaning over to grab a t-shirt and boxers.

"You're a piece of work, you really are. I didn't assume we would get back together but I thought at the very least we could have a proper conversation? Or was I just a ride 'cause you weren't getting anywhere with anyone in that dive?" he accused coldly.

His callous summary of the situation brought Teeny some relief. *Still a prick,* she surmised.

He rubbed his hand over his mouth realising he had overstepped and tried to lower his voice.

"Maybe it was proper goodbye?" Teeny offered, deciding to ignore his comment.

"Goodbye," he repeated, laughing sarcastically. "Aye, that's it, a nice wee goodbye before you disappear into the sunset again. What's it going to be this time, sweetheart; six months, a year? Before you come back to fuck up everyone's peace again?" he added as he put on his trousers from the end of the bed and walked past her to the kitchen.

"Meaning?" Teeny challenged, following him.

"Don't be cute, Colette. You love all the drama of it. The fighting, the making up, the chase, the chaos. It's like you're addicted to it?" he scoffed at her then took a long drink of water from the glass he'd poured for himself.

"Fuck off!" She laughed out in a high-pitched squeak. "The *fighting*? Is that how you described it? You're sick," she added and the words tasted like acid in her mouth.

Without flinching, he said, "Well, on your advice, I went to a counsellor. A different one. *She* helped me realise that I keep choosing women who need 'fixing' or 'saving'. Unstable damsels in distress seems to be my type." He half shrugged and continued, "And I didn't want to believe it about you and I should have known better to stay away knowing you were back but I just wanted to see you, to speak to you and then you practically drag me into bed? Now you're just disappearing again like I'm some cheap one-night stand. Real classy. Serves me right for trying to help," he said and casually set about setting up the cafetiere.

Teeny felt glued to the floor, rage was burning up her legs and into her chest and as she rested her hands against the bar stool in front of her, she resisted the urge to pick it up and throw it across the breakfast bar at him. She pictured him in the counsellor's office, an attractive woman she guessed, taking her notes and him, filling her with all the shite she'd want to hear to cure him and him omitting any facts that would mean him needing to take ownership of his abusive and aggressive natures. Teeny nodded as she held onto the stool for support.

"You did help, Mark. Really. Please be sure to tell your counsellor that this damsel took a kick in really well and just fucking adored sweating anytime her phone would ring or vibrate unannounced in case 'her saviour' read it first and wanted to quiz her about it for hours. You were a real hero, cheers." She gave a sarcastic 'OK' sign and roughly shoved the stool away from her letting it clatter to the ground.

"You done?" he asked raising his eyebrow as if she were a petulant child throwing a tantrum.

"Absolutely, aye. Goodbye, Mark," she said as she turned away and walked down the hall.

"Aye, cheerio," he responded a little more dejectedly than he maybe intended to, Teeny thought.

Teeny hesitated at Jen's door on the way out and thought about knocking. She decided against it and made her way into the High Street. She could perhaps meet Jen later to discuss her latest fuck up but not like this, not when she would still hear his footsteps and still had his sweat clinging to her. She bought herself a roll and a bottle of juice and took a seat on one of the benches to try and combat the nausea from her hangover. The High Street would be busy soon and she didn't want to risk bumping into anyone like this. She jumped on the bus and made her way back to her parents and as each stop got closer to her destination, she knew it wasn't just her hangover making her stomach churn and mouth dry.

The kitchen was empty when she walked into the back door. She could smell burnt toast and fried bacon and sausage so knew her parents were still home.

"Hello? It's me. Mum? Dad?" she called, unsure if she was even welcome after the embarrassment she caused them the night before.

"Through here, wee yin," her mum answered.

As Teeny walked through into the living room she was surprised to find both her parents. Alec normally slept much later. Denise was still wearing her lilac housecoat and had been crying, Alec sat on the floor in front of her, holding her

187

hand. The scene immediately made Teeny panic. Had her actions caused her mother to hurt herself, to take all her pills again, or worse?

"Mum, what's wrong, what's happened?" she asked in a panic-stricken whisper, afraid of the answer.

Denise simply put out her hand offering Teeny to take it. She gingerly stepped towards them, taking it and sitting down.

"Mum?" she repeated.

"Is it true, darlin'? About Mark? They two doon the pub? What they did? Your dad thought maybe you had done something to yourself when you hadn't come home and he told me what you told him last night. Is it true?" she asked, letting her voice pitch at the end, new tears stinging her throat.

Teeny squeezed her hand tighter but looked away, towards the door. The weight of her experiences hanging in the room, trying to shove her down into the floor. She nodded.

"All of it," she said quietly.

"Oh God," Denise cried louder and released Teeny's grasp so she could sob into her own hands. "You should have told your dad, Teeny, he would have fucking killed them. You should have told me," Denise pleaded in between sobs.

Teeny looked between her mother, her father then the floor. Alec may have told Denise the truth, but not the whole version. He needed to preserve the version where he still had the chance of being the hero. Teeny would let him. The truth would knot in his own stomach and sit heavily on his conscious. She didn't want to bring more pain into the room, into her mother's eyes.

"It doesn't matter, Mum, really. It's done. I'm-I'm OK now," she lied, choking back her own tears. The three of them sat in silence for a long time, letting the unknown truths fall into the chasm between them.

Later that weekend, she had met Jen for coffee and after ten minutes or so of small talk, Jen cut through the pleasantries.

"OK, are you going to tell me what's being going on or we just gonna talk shit about Netflix some more?" She half smiled.

Teeny sighed, cursing her friend's incredible intuition. She told her how she had come back to try and piece together her life since she had just fled at Christmas. She wanted a true fresh start, not to feel like she was in hiding or had unfinished business. Instead, she had outed herself in the most catastrophic way changing the dynamics of her relationships with her parents, with Darren, with any regular in the pub forever.

"Oh, and I slept with Mark," she added casually at the end of her story.

Jen had sat with both hands 'round her cup listening to Teeny talk at 100 miles an hour, trying to get the information out of her soul as quickly and seamlessly as possible. She didn't want to interrupt Teeny for clarification so just let her speak at her chosen pace. When she was done, she sat back, trying to absorb even some of it.

"Jesus!" was all she said.

"So, you want to just go back to chatting shite about Netflix after all or will I keep talking about how much I made a cunt of myself in less than 24 hours?" Teeny said mocking herself as her eyes welled up.

Jen reached out and held her friend's hand.

"Hey, listen. It maybe didn't play out like you would have liked but babe, that took serious balls to even acknowledge it out loud like that. And fuck, maybe this is a good start to having a proper relationship with your folks?"

Teeny scoffed at the prospect but knew Jen's heart was in the right place.

There was no going back now, the genie was out of the bottle.

"But how did Mark end up in the mix here?" Jen asked.

Teeny gave her the play by play of how he had turned up and then had the nerve to turn it on her like she was the toxic one between the two of them.

"Why the fuck did I go back there? Why did I sleep with him?" Teeny shook her head reprimanding herself.

"Um, 'cause the only time he's nice to you and looks after your needs is when he's between your legs? He might be toxic, but shit, he's great in bed. All the good sociopaths are." Jen laughed, raising her eyebrows and sipped her coffee.

Teeny felt cheap but recognised there was a truth in what she was saying. She always felt safe and at peace when they were physically close. He was never cruel or unkind to her during these moments so they became the moments she clung to, sought out even. She sighed at the simple revelation.

"Sorry, that was overstepping. Sometimes, you just want to feel good so you go to where your body remembers feeling good. Don't feel shitty about it, you got him told, that's something. If it were me? I'd still report him so the next girl doesn't find out the hard way though, you know?" Jen finished as she started to rip up the sugar sachets and tip the tiny snowflakes into her empty cup.

Teeny sighed. This wasn't the first time it had occurred to her to report the abuse to the police nor the first time Jen had urged her to do so. She explained to Teeny how it wouldn't necessarily need to be a terrifying experience in a courtroom, it could be very discreet and she'd be well looked after. Her actions would mean other women would be able to find out what he was capable of. She'd thought about it for herself. Maybe his ex-partner, Lauren, had been to the police when they were together. Teeny couldn't bring herself to make the first call. Guilt for women who didn't even exist in Mark's life yet thudded in her chest and pounded in her head.

"I can't. They wouldn't believe me. It's been too long." She started to panic at the thought of the questioning.

He would outwit her and make her look ridiculous. She'd already dropped a bombshell of abuse in public and would now feel its scars for the rest of her life. She didn't want justice; she couldn't face the weight of the responsibility to give a warning outlet to other women. She wasn't ready, she just wanted to be free.

Jen must have sensed Teeny's drifting thoughts as she interrupted them gently, "Tell me if I'm out of order, babe, but this might be a good time to think about getting some proper help. I mean I'm all ears but you've been through some real shit and maybe the best thing is talking about it. Working through it?" Jen suggested while rubbing her hand over Teeny's wrist.

Teeny nodded and sipped at her now cold coffee. "Aye, maybe," she replied and continued to nod.

It could have been the caffeine or her emotions catching up with her from the weekend's events but Teeny's stomach was in knots. Jen had left her to head to her first class with a promise of meeting up in the next couple of weeks since they'd left the conversation on quite a dark note. Teeny wandered down the street past the hall Jen was heading in to teach. She couldn't concentrate and her mind was swimming. She took a seat on a small grass verge which led up to a bridge over the burn. Teeny listened to the soothing trickling of the water. She timed her breath to it so she could regain some control over her body, deliberately feeling the damp grass below her hands as she did so.

"I'm OK, I'm going to be OK, it's OK," she rehearsed to herself.

For much of her life, she had been able to keep her emotions to herself, her story to herself and it made her appear aloof or enigmatic perhaps. But now, she felt like everyone knew her story, who she was or at least the version they had pieced together. She felt exposed. A fraud. A victim.

"I'm OK, I'm going to be OK, it's OK," she repeated. She looked at her phone to check the time and realised the date. In the next week or so, it would be the year anniversary since she and Mark first kissed that night in the pub. One year. Teeny suddenly laughed to herself. She felt as if she had aged maybe five years in that time and had lived at least three lifetimes worth of drama. But the calendar would correct her and confirm she was still only 21. The world seemed different now, bigger somehow. Teeny took a large, purposeful mouthful of air as if trying to cure hiccups and gave a long guttural sigh to clear her lungs, breathe cleaner. She realised the derailed train that was her mind had never fully come back onto the tracks, only careened further down the bank, still moving only further off course. She needed to take some proper time to figure herself out and heal and perhaps start a new, more peaceful journey.

Mark

"Yep, aye aye, I'm still here. I heard you. Football at 6 for the wee man, Grace's dance thing has been cancelled. I heard you, see you soon love you, love you, bye."

Mark hurriedly hit the end call button on the Bluetooth in his car so he could roll down the window and hear better. Hear her voice and laughter as she waddled after the curly haired toddler who was running away from her. She stopped to stand and rub her stomach and shield her eyes from the lowering sun. He instinctively shuffled down in the driver's seat to avoid being seen but she hadn't noticed and wasn't likely to; it was a different car he drove now. It'd been nearly ten years since he last saw Colette and it made him feel edgy, nervous and shameful.

"Mark, can we go over now? My game starts soon, I need to get my boots on," his stepson whined from the back seat.

"In a minute pal, I just need to answer a couple of emails, OK? And your sister's dance class has been cancelled so we don't need to wait about for her after, good eh?"

This seemed to appease him and he went back to his game on his phone as Mark pretended to read emails on his, watching Colette in her new life, willing her to walk away quicker to avoid any interaction but also a curiosity of wanting her to linger so he could see what she looked like now.

Her hair was longer and lighter, she wore a long summery dress that clung to her pregnant bump and her smile as she watched the wee girl running about was glorious. Her other half, he assumed, picked the toddler up and she squealed with delight as he helicoptered her around the park then released her to go running towards the slide. He watched with familiar jealousy creeping to his fists as the guy stood behind her rubbing her belly and whispering in her ear. He breathed slowly as he flexed his fingers and looked down to his pretend emails but the screen had locked again on his phone, as it came back to life, the screensaver of his wife and his stepchildren pulled him back to reality of who he was now and not the man he was then. It had taken too long to get here and his shame made him look away from the faces on the phone. Would they have anything to do with him if they knew? The gravity of how much had changed in ten years for him and for Colette by the looks of things was striking. He physically winced as the remembered their last interaction, the catalyst to becoming the person he was today.

"Mark. Mark? Are you alright, do you want to continue?" the counsellor had asked, interrupting his wandering thoughts. He had been carefully dodging questions for his last couple of sessions about any 'underlying issues he may have' which made him so angry. He'd bullshitted her so far that he threw glasses and punched walls but never a person, never a woman. Colette's words had stung him and sat heavy on his conscious the last couple of days. She looked as though she really hated him. There was no coming back from this now. He couldn't know for sure what the punters in that shithole knew or what that smug prick Darren had told them. He felt like the weight of her words was compressing around him like a vice making his ribs feel tight and his head dizzy. As he reached out for the flimsy plastic cup of water, his hand trembled.

"I'm…I don't think I'm a good person, a good partner I mean." He swallowed hard after he spoke as if the truth he wanted to share sat like a golf ball in his throat.

The counsellor stretched her shoulders back and twiddled her pen between her fingers. "Can you tell me a bit more about that?" she asked.

Not a loaded question, but a free space, for Mark to come clean and share his inner most shameful moments. He couldn't bring himself to describe the details, his new spark of honesty only took him so far.

"I lifted my hands, I checked her phone a lot, I frightened her," were the buzz phrases he managed to reveal to secure some kind of understanding from the counsellor. To get some actual help, not help for the version of himself he was painting. Revisiting the scenes in his head made his stomach flip now. He knew she could have gone to the police but didn't. He knew she could tell family and friends but didn't. No show of loyalty or love ever seemed to be enough. It made his insides boil anytime she looked too done up to go to work or spent too long on her phone.

He didn't know what to say to her when she threw the barstool over the week before. He thought she was going to throw it at him. She looked truly disgusted with him and he'd been unable to shake the image in his mind since. When he got back to the car after the session, he held onto the wheel and gripped it until his fingers hurt so he could feel something other than the cold shame in his gut and regret tingling at his neck. He felt so exposed like at any minute the police would turn up outside his car, knock on the window and take him away for being such a bastard. He finally recognised he needed proper help. Help to control his anger and unpack his insecurities that made him want to act on jealous, unprovoked impulses. It only made him miserable and alone. He had tried counselling a couple of times before, usually on the behest of his partners; Colette, Lauren, women too in love to leave but too frightened to stay. It had never worked out before because he felt judged. It made him feel ugly and raw. Today felt different. It felt as though if he didn't speak about it, the guilt would suffocate him. He wanted to be a better man than he had been, better than the man he was pretending to be.

"I need to get over there, Mark, I've just seen Luke and Caleb go past, I'm going to be late!" His stepson brought him back to the present, reminding him they needed to get out the car.

"Right pal, sorry, get your boots on," he apologised as he put his phone in his pocket and lifted his jacket from the passenger seat and watched the silhouette of her family walk to the other side of the car park.

It made so much sense to him now that he and Colette didn't work out as a couple, couldn't work. Both so insecure and damaged in their own way clinging to the desire to fix and heal each other and build something real together, beyond lust and excitement. Mark loved his wife, very much, and had no desire to be with anyone else. He felt at home with her and if he ever felt angry or impulsive or out of control, which was so rare these days, she spoke with understanding and strength to help him come back down and ground himself.

Still, he felt a sadness looking at Colette now, as a proper grown up which seemed strange in itself. A feeling of sadness that he couldn't make her glow or laugh like that. It only felt as though it were another reminder that they were never 'meant to be' but perhaps, meant to be a lesson to one another. Part of each other's journey in healing themselves.

He took a couple of deep breaths before finally stepping out of the car and smiled affectionately at his stepson who only looked confused and annoyed as he handed him his phone for safe keeping and ran towards the football field to his waiting friends. Mark allowed himself one final look at the most dramatic chapter in his life as she carefully climbed into the driver's seat and put on her sunglasses with her music instantly blaring out of the windows, which made him smile as they drove off in the opposite direction.

Colette

It was a job Colette had been putting off for weeks. Clearing the loft.

"Why the fuck do we keep so much SHITE up here?" She laughed to herself moving boxes of receipts and dining room chairs from a set disused many years before.

"You shouting on me?" a distant voice from below called up to her.

She peered out the hatch. "No? I did shout 'shite' though 'cause the loft is fucking full of it. Mostly yours by the way," she said in a mockingly annoyed tone.

"Listen, it's better to have it and not need it than—"

"…need it and not have it," she finished tersely, interrupting her husband. "It's hoardy is what it is, honey. Half of this is going to the tip, it's not coming with us. I'm not doing this again if we ever move in the future," she scolded with her eyebrows raised, to signal this wasn't up for debate.

"Aye, fair enough. You wanting a hand? I've got 20 minutes or so before I need to collect the kids from my mum's?" Ross asked.

Colette looked at his tired, paint splattered face with plaster caked on his knuckles.

Her husband was by no means a DIY expert but had taken up the mantle of tarting up all the minor repairs to their home before they sold it and moved to their new, much bigger house. Her job was to clear the loft and she had studiously procrastinated for far too long yet here he was still offering to help.

She smiled at him and shook her head. "Nah, you get yourself showered, I'll crack on and sorry for being a moany bitch, I just wish I'd picked the painting and plastering, it would have been easier!" She laughed and he blew her a sarcastic kiss before heading through to their bedroom to use the shower.

She shifted the boxes and bags around to what would just be dropped down the hatch to go to the tip and what would need properly boxed to transport in a couple of weeks' time.

She started to condense the bags of Christmas decorations so there would be less to move and thought this would be a good idea for the miscellaneous junk at the back wall. She boxed up bags of baby clothes, birthday cards and rainbow posters with superhero nurses and doctors poorly drawn in the middle. She found a shoebox that had been taped up but the tape had folded back on itself from the way a large bag had been tossed haphazardly on it. The minute she opened it, she knew what it was; this was all her trinkets and memories from her younger years. She stroked the golden imprint of the title on her now well-read copy of *The Catcher in the Rye*. She found some baby photographs of herself her mother gave her and a couple of her old journals. These were mostly hand scrawled for her eyes only so it didn't really matter what she wrote. She had taken the advice in counselling to write her feelings, write about her experiences, her rage, her fears.

"Allow it to flow like a stream of consciousness, don't overthink it," the counsellor would say.

She was grateful she used pen and paper and that her handwriting was so terrible as she didn't want to particularly visit those thoughts and judgements of herself as a young 25-year-old woman figuring life out all those years ago. At the back of the journal, there was a hand typed letter which she recognised straight away. She remembered typing it, excruciatingly slowly in the library. She'd been given 'the homework assignment' in her latest counselling session and wanted to make use of the keyboarding skills course she was taking. She thought it would be good practice for her course she was due to start studying later in the year which involved far more essay and report writing than her accounting course ever had. The assignment was to write a letter to her younger self, to offer words of wisdom and encouragement that she perhaps wished she'd heard at that particular time in her life; she chose to write to her 21-year-old self. Colette hadn't cried like this for a long time. She cried when they took their beloved pet to be put to sleep, she cried when their son dislocated his shoulder at the park and the doctor had to roughly pop it back in while he screamed into her chest and she cried softly while holding her heart in her dimly lit loft surrounded in boxes as she reread the letter and reflected on how much had changed for her over the years, how happy she was now and how desperately sad she was when she was still so young.

Dear Colette,

I love you. You should know that first. You might not hear it a lot the now or for real, out loud for a long long time. But I do. I love you. You're frightened. Of what you said, what you did, what they did and what he did. That's OK, it was frightening. But please, don't be scared of yourself. Don't be scared of your own shadow because you can really do it, you can move on (and you will!). You're going to be OK (keep saying it when you're anxious because it works – you will be OK). You're going to be happier than you ever thought possible and all because you're going to do the work. You're going to take charge of your life and choose yourself more and more often and before long, it will feel easy and right and seamless instead of awkward or like you're imposing on others by demanding your needs are met. You're important and I love you (did I say that already?).

There is still so much of the world to see and so much to do. You'll soon cry tears of joy for the first time and you'll fall in love with yourself and learn about yourself all over again. It'll take time and you'll always need to work on yourself in one way or another but facing your mind won't seem so scary anymore and you'll be able to carry out conversations with eejits without wanting to glass them or throw shit at them ('cause that only makes you more mad chook). I know this sounds nuts and don't worry, you don't start smoking Jen's 'special cigarettes' by the way, you just learn to like yourself better and love yourself properly and that will attract good people into your life. Very good people. You'll fall in love again with someone who won't frighten or disrespect you, or hurt you. You'll know the difference, you'll be ready.

In the meantime, please be kind to yourself and remember;

You are smart
You are funny
You are caring
You are loving
You are loved.

Lots of love, slightly older and wiser Colette xxx